The
OUTCAST
TAYA RUNE

Outcast

Cover Design: Sweet 15 Designs
For information contact :
purplerealmpublishing@gmail.com
ISBN: 978-1-922604-19-4 (ebook)
ISBN : 978-1-922604-20-0 (paperback)
ISBN : 978-1-922604-38-5 (audio)
First Edition: May 2022

Purple Realm Publishing

RIGHT TO RULE SERIES

USA TODAY BESTSELLING AUTHOR
TAYA RUNE

Taya's Steamy Books

Steamy Contemporary

Champagne Resolutions

War of Hearts

Bewitching Twisted Fairytales

The Charming Thief

Fantasy Romance
The Right To Rule Series

Outcast

Lethal

Fatal

Betrayal

Denial
(Coming January 2024)

<u>Paranormal Mystery Romance</u>
Enchanted Underworld
Weapons of the Fae Queen Series

The Warlock's Lair

The Oracle's Court

The Nymph's Realm

The Dragon's Garden
(Coming 2nd November 2023)

Check out her website for all her current works.

tayarune.com

Newsletter

To receive up-to-date information, news and exclusive
offers online please sign up for the
Taya Rune newsletter.

https://www.tayarune.com/subscribe

Content Warning

If you are concerned about content, please check Taya's website for a list of warnings for all of her books.
It can be found under the 'Books' tab.

tayarune.com

'The poor little duckling did not know where to turn. How he grieved over his own ugliness, and how sad he was! The poor creature was mocked and laughed at by the whole henyard.'

The Ugly Duckling
by
Hans Christian Anderson

Chapter 1

"I know you're in here, Creeper." His voice was soft, almost crooning, as he stalked the darkened spaces of the basement. A small amount of light filtered through the broken slats of a vent, showing the swirling dust motes that had been disturbed as he searched.

Kahlahnni held her breath as his shadowed figure moved through the shaft of light and closer to her hiding place. She peered into the gloom, trying to keep track of her tormentor.

"You can't hide forever." His footsteps and passing shadow told her that he was moving away from her hiding place. "Just give me your bread and I'll go," he reasoned. They both knew he was lying.

The stale bread she held in her small hand was almost inedible, but it was hers. Kahlahnni needed her rations just as much as he did and she wasn't about to give them up to a bully, no matter how many times he tortured her. He always had to catch her first, and every month she grew more adept at avoiding him. Kahlahnni's deep brown eyes grew hard as she tore a piece of bread off with her teeth and chewed on the dry crust; simply so if he caught her he would still have less bread to steal. She knew it was spiteful, but she was beyond caring.

Kahlahnni was nine, lived in a boarding house that took in orphans of the area, and worked from dawn till dusk in the laundry room to pay her way and she had had one friend in the world until Cellecia had taken a job at the Lord's estate house as the second cook and had left. Now Lahnni had no one to protect her and that had been proven when Ambrosse had attacked her hair with a pair of shears in the kitchen one morning. She had managed to avoid him and his demands for her food for a sennight prior and he had punished her for it.

As the tasteless bread turned to a hard lump as she chewed, she tensed her cramped muscles for a few moments in the hope it would relieve some of the discomfort she was experiencing, curled in a ball, hidden on the top of the cupboard. Kahalanni always found it astounding that no one ever looked up. Ambrosse continued to call out his pet nickname for her as if that was going to make her answer. "Creeper?" he said softly.

He had given her the horrid name when he had found her attempting to slink past his door one morning with a shiny green apple in her hand, given to her by the then-cook, Cellecia, who had befriended her when Kahlahnni worked in the kitchen before graduating to the laundry at age seven. Ambrosse was the resident bully, tall for his thirteen years, powerfully built already, and he found happiness in hurting and intimidating the children who lived in the boarding house.

Kahlahnni had always managed to stay out of his way by being quiet and hiding behind others, but she looked different to everyone else, and even at the age of five she had understood that it was not a good thing to be anything other than ordinary. Ambrosse had opened his door just as Kahlahnni had managed to get by and had immediately spotted the shiny green object in her hand. She recalled the moment vividly. "Don't think I don't see you, Creeper. Always hiding, trying not to stand out with that ugly dark hair and those strange brown eyes. You watch everyone; it's really creepy." He had fake shuddered. His pale gray eyes had settled onto the hand that held her apple. "I think for looking so hideous you should give me the apple." The smile he had given her at that moment could still send chills of fear down her spine. Kahlahnni had shaken her head, too scared to speak. Even though Ambrosse was several years older and much bigger than her, she had decided at that moment that she was not going to just give in. Something inside her told her that she was not worthless just because she was different. Ambrosse had held out his hand and waited. "You will give it to me or I will take it," he had warned.

Again, Kahlahnni had shaken her head, her grip on the apple tightening slightly.

Without warning, Ambrosse had raised his hand and slapped her sharply across her cheek. Kahlahnni had fallen to the hard wooden floor and the apple rolled out of her hand. Tears came to her eyes as she had held her hand to her stinging cheek. She watched him, but didn't move. Ambrosse had sneered at her, picked up the apple where it had rolled, and had taken a large bite. Then, with a measured tone that told her her life was about to become even more miserable than it already was, said, "Thank you, Creeper. I look forward to eating your breakfast every morning."

That had been half a year ago and it had become a game of cat and mouse. One Kahlahnni loathed and Ambrosse seemed to thrive on. The young girl had always been good at hiding in plain sight, but she had become a master of it. It was as if she had developed a sixth sense to when Ambrosse was feeling particularly pugnacious, and at those moments she would simply hand over her food rather than risk being hurt like the last time he had managed to corner her and she had refused to hand over her morning meal. There was now a tiny scar on her neck to remind her what he was capable of even when she didn't look in the mirror to see her missing hair.

As she lay in the dark, waiting for Ambrosse to give up looking for her for another day, the memory of the last time he had cornered her and she had been bold enough to defy him rose unbidden, and though she tried to push it aside it still came. It had been a typical morning in the boarding house. It was cold, as the sun had not risen to burn the mist away yet, and Kahlahnni remembered her hands had hurt from the combination of the cold and being sore from spending the day before scrubbing dirty sheets in freezing water with lyre soap that made her skin crack and weep. She had spent a few extra moments in the kitchen by the fire, waiting for her thin gruel to be ready. No one spoke to her and she tried to ignore the ones who actively cast suspicious looks in her direction, like she couldn't be trusted because she looked different. Her only friend, Cellecia, had left a month prior and it was only then did Kahlahnni realize the kitchen was no longer a haven for her.

Ambrosse had arrived to collect his meal and Kahlahnni tried not to shudder at the memory of the look of triumph in his pale eyes when he had spotted her. Fear had risen unbidden, and even now she still couldn't understand how she had known that day would be different. "Creeper, have you been avoiding me?" His tone was mocking as he stood too close to her.

Kahlahnni had not answered. She had turned away from him and was grateful to discover the gruel was ready. The young kitchen hand indicated she could come and take her portion. Ambrosse had followed close behind and in that instant Kahlahnni decided to eat in the kitchen. Typically she would hide somewhere to eat, but he had already found her and she wasn't safe if she left the adults. How wrong she had been.

As she had settled onto the edge of the large table they used to eat at and prepare the food, she tried to make herself as small and inconspicuous as possible, all the more wishing that Cellecia had been there. Kahlahnni had kept her head down and hurriedly eaten the lumpy, thin porridge in the hope she finished well before Ambrosse and could get away and to the laundry room, where she would remain until the day had finished. He was assigned to the cooper of the small town they lived in so he left every day to earn his keep. Ambrosse had sat beside her and leaned in to speak so no one would hear. The basement faded completely as she was drawn into the memory. "Remember to leave some for me, Creeper."

Kahlahnni kept her head down and continued eating. Fear gripped her, but she refused to show it; she just needed to eat quicker and get out of there. Why did no one hear her heart beating?

"I'm warning you," his voice hissed in her ear.

She scraped the last of the gruel from her bowl and shoveled it in her mouth, looking sideways at Ambrosse to see his reaction. Even terrified she was defiant. He stood, leaving his bowl half-finished and Kahlahnni's ears filled with the sound of her rushing blood. What was he going to do? She sat still, wishing for someone to intervene, but no one did. Two children were not worth noticing, especially the one that didn't fit in. Ambrosse moved behind her and she slowly felt him take hold of her waist-length, rich brown hair, and twist it tightly in his fist. He leaned over so he could whisper in her ear. "You are revolting to look at, and not wanted." He held her hair tight so she couldn't move. "Stay still or I will cut you," he warned. The word 'cut' reverberated through her. What was he about to do? "Speak a word and you will regret it." His words were final and she knew he meant the threat. Whatever it was, she had to endure it or he would hunt her down and the punishment would be far greater. He had proven that on numerous occasions.

Ambrosse tugged on her hair several times and she remained silent and still, only whimpering slightly when she heard the click of the shears coming together as he hacked off the first pieces of her thick curls. Tears had come to her brown eyes, but she sat there too horrified by what was happening to utter a word. He was a hideous bully to all the children, but he targeted her the most—why did the adults do nothing about it? As the shears came close to her ear she had flinched, and Ambrosse had nicked her neck with the shears. "Oh dear, now you are bleeding." He said it as if he had not been the cause, and with a calm that made Kahlahnni ill, he had bent down and licked the blood that had risen to the surface on the shallow cut. The feeling was vile; his wet tongue and hot breath on her neck were terrifying, and at that moment Kahlahnni wished Ambrosse dead.

An explosion of color followed the angry thought and an image of a fully grown Ambrosse; his gray eyes wide with horror and his mouth distorted in a silent scream appeared in her head. Dried blood caked one side of his face and it was clear he was in great pain. The image scared her so much she yelped, finally drawing the attention of the cook. "What are you two doing?"

With a look of confidence, Ambrosse held up the wad of curls he had cut off. "She asked me to cut her hair so she doesn't stand out as much. You don't like being noticed do you, Kahlahnni?" He made it all appear so reasonable.

All she could do was blink at the cook, willing him to understand that her silence did not mean consent. "Well, you shouldn't be doing it in here. Finish up, throw that hair in the fire, and get out of here, you two."

How could they not see how distressed she was? *They don't want to*, her inner voice whispered.

"I am finished," Ambrosse declared and moved to throw her curls in the fire.

Kahlahnni took that moment to make her escape and bolted for the door and ran to the safety of the laundry room where she had spent the afternoon sobbing as she wrung out nightdresses for the local convent. She had always secretly loved her hair, even though everyone thought it strange to have such dark tresses, it had made her feel special. Now it was gone and she looked even uglier than she normally did. Why couldn't she just fit in?

The lump of bread caught in her throat and pulled her back into the present. Kahlahnni couldn't stop it. A tiny cough came from her as her throat tried to cope with the round ball of dough she was attempting to swallow. She heard Ambrosse spin and held her breath.

"Ah, Creeper, I knew you were in here," he gloated. Ambrosse moved to stand in the weak light and she could see triumph on his teenage pimpled face. His golden-red hair glinted in the sun and it only then occurred to her that they were both late to work. The sun had risen.

Kahlahnni watched him turn slowly in place before he stopped and looked in the direction of her cupboard. She willed him to keep turning, but instead, he moved toward her, stepping out of the light and allowing him to hide in the shadows again. She felt the wobble of the cupboard as he yanked both the doors open. With instinct born of desperation, the need to eat her bread evaporated and she hurled it to the other side of the basement, willing it to hit something that would create enough noise to draw him away.

Her plan worked, and it hit something that hit something else and several things toppled onto the floor, causing enough noise for him to rush to the other side of the room and allow her to quietly ease herself off the top of the cupboard and onto the boxes she had stacked up behind it to climb her way to the top. She paused on the second box as everything went quiet again. There were two boxes to go before she was on the ground and could make a dash for the stairs. Kahlahnni couldn't decide if she was more anxious about being caught by Ambrosse or being late for work and what those consequences would be—she had no where to go if she was kicked out of the boarding house.

Kahlahnni felt trapped in her choices. Deciding that having a place to live, no matter how hostile, was better than living on the streets, she put her foot gingerly on the next box. It creaked and Kahlahnni almost cried out in despair. There was no other way but for her to hope that she was quicker at escaping than he was at finding her.

As her foot hit the uneven packed earth, Ambrosse materialized before her and towered over her glowering. "Told you I would find you."

Kahlahnni's ankle twisted and she fell to the ground, landing heavily at his feet, causing him to laugh. "You truly are worthless."

At that moment the door at the top of the stairs was opened and light poured in. A voice called out, "You in here, Lahnni?"

Kahlahnni began to cry, she recognized the voice and no one but Cellecia used that nickname. "Yes."

"Well, come on. There is a position at the Lord's manor for someone to look after his elderly mother. I told them you would be perfect for the role."

"I am coming." Kahlahnni wiped her nose with her dirty sleeve and made to stand up, putting her hand out to pull herself up on the side of the box. Instead, she felt her hand be grasped by Ambrosse and she couldn't snatch it back in time. "Allow me," he spoke grandly.

He hauled her to her feet, but before he let go he twisted her thumb and they both heard something snap in the silence. "A parting gift." He bent over the hand like a gentleman and kissed it before dropping it.

The pain was excruciating and Kahlahnni whimpered as she cradled her thumb to her chest. Images flooded into her mind, images of Ambrosse covered in blood again, his mouth wide in a silent scream, but this time the background was filled with flames and falling debris. Then everything went black, and all that there was

was a vacant-eyed Ambrosse lying in a twisted, unnatural position. The image no longer scared her—it fueled her. Kahlahnni stepped closer so they were inches from touching and she gave him her sincerest smile. "I have seen you die, and it will be what you deserve."

Chapter 2

A single strand of her dark brown hair had escaped from its bonnet and Kahlahnni quickly shoved it back under the protective material. Over the years she had come to serve the Lady Aisllyn, she had learned that if her hair was covered she was less likely to be harassed by the other staff or visitors to the Manor House. Her deep brown eyes didn't draw as much attention as she kept them averted when people were near, while her thick, curly mid-length brown hair tended to be a beacon for people who felt superior and were afraid of anyone who looked different from themselves.

A bell in the kitchen announced that Lady Aisllyn was awake and ready to break her fast. Lahnni patted her head to make certain her hair was all hidden as the cook put the warm scones and fruit preserve on the heavy silver tray for the Lady of the house. A small goblet of mead was also placed on the tray next to a linen napkin. The greasy-haired cook clapped his chubby hands to let Lahnni know she could take the tray, rather than tell her. No one spoke to her unless they had to. It made for a lonely existence, but she was grateful she wasn't tormented every day nor did she have to sneak her food or be hyper-aware of who was near her.

Her friend, Cellecia, had only been at the Manor House with Lahnni a year when her husband had returned from serving in the King's Navy, as the war for the Islands of Lobbregath had been fought and again won. It was the third time in as many decades that the nation of Segarris had had to protect their outer lying colonies from the marauders of Trioswa who continued to mount attempts to seize control of the trading routes and out lying islands off the South East coast of Segarris. Cellecia's husband had returned a hero and had been given a large enough pay out that he was able to open a small bakery, where his wife could use her cooking skills and he could help. The last Kahlahnni had heard, Cellecia was pregnant with their third child, but that had been overheard gossip six months ago from someone who had returned from town.

Being careful not to spill the mead, Lahnni picked up the tray and walked out of the hot kitchen and into the colder corridors that ran along the back of the large manor for the servants to use and not be seen. Though, not for the first time, Lahnni wondered why it mattered when the only noble in residence was Lady Aisllyn and she rarely came out of her room. It would be quicker, and the Lady would have less need to complain that her meal had cooled if Lahnni could use the main hallways to get to the master suite.

She took the narrow, squeaky stairs up to the small landing and turned into a large, richly furnished corridor. Lahnni placed the tray on the small table outside Lady Aisllyn's door and tapped three times as she had been taught when she had first come to serve five years ago. She counted to ten and then opened the door, picked up the tray again, and made her way into the darkened room.

With years of practice, Lahnni quietly set about preparing for the ancient woman to rise and begin her day. Once the tray was safely placed on the small table that served as a writing desk, as well as the Lady's preferred place to eat, Lahnni moved to open the heavy drapes and allow the weak morning light to peer through the vines that covered half the window. The manor was overrun with vines. Lady Aisllyn declared that she liked the look of the green tentacles climbing the blue stone walls and she always muttered that the world had forgotten about her and she wanted to forget about it in return. Once the curtains were tied back, Lahnni moved to the drapes that hung around the four-poster bed. She kept her eyes averted as she completed her task and secured the curtains to the bedposts.

Lahnni frowned as she hurried to pick up the soft lilac dressing robe that had been draped over the end of the bed the night before when Lady Aisllyn had retired for the evening. It was unusual for it to be on the floor.

Usually by now there was some movement from the bed. She meekly cleared her throat as she moved up to the top end of the bed, hoping that would wake Lady Aisllyn, as Lahnni guessed the old woman had fallen back to sleep. Steeling herself, Lahnni spoke her first words for the day. "Lady Aisllyn, your meal is here." She paused and waited for the brusque mannered, thin voice of her employer to admonish her for speaking out of turn, but nothing happened. "Lady?" Lahnni said it with a little more conviction. Again nothing.

With reluctance, Kahlahnni lifted her eyes to check on the old woman. A small gasp escaped her as she looked at the withered body lying at an odd angle like she had been reaching for something and had collapsed. Lahnni followed where Lady Aisllyn's hand was reaching and came to the conclusion that she had probably rung the kitchen bell to have Lahnni bring up her meal, but had then died as she was moving to lie back down. Her watery, pale blue eyes were open and her mouth slack. Without thinking, Lahnni reached out to touch the bony hand to confirm to herself that Lady Aisllyn was in fact deceased. The hand was warm to touch, but there was no other response. Her mind didn't present her with images as it usually did when she touched a person.

Over the years, her gift, as she had come to call it, grew more powerful, but was spasmodic in the way it behaved. It had been distressing until she realized that if she didn't touch anyone with skin to skin contact the visions rarely came, and only when she was overly emotional. When her cycles had started, she had begun to feel the emotions of those around her and she had become frightened that she was losing her grip on reality, but with no one to con- fide in she had had to battle through until she realized her own emotions were affecting her gift. Lahnni was now about to turn fifteen and her cycles had settled about six months ago, giving her the chance to figure out that she became more emotional just before they arrived, and that extra emotion triggered her vulnerability to more powerful visions. If she kept her equilibrium, the over- whelming and sometimes terrifying emotional backlash was kept under control. Between understanding that if she remained calm, kept a tight rein on her emotions, and didn't touch anyone, she could almost pretend she was normal, but her exterior would always betray her. Sometimes Kahlahnni would go days without speaking to anyone and she was unsure if they even noticed. *Is this the time to feel sorry for yourself? Get it together*, she told herself.

Giving the hand a gentle squeeze, Lahnni whispered to the woman that had rescued her from the boarding house, "Thank you. It has been lonely, but I have been safe." A memory of Ambrosse's cruel smile flashed in her mind's eye and she shuddered; that boy's face would forever haunt her.

Lahnni reached over and tugged on the green bell pull twice to summon the housekeeper. She then checked the room to make sure everything was in order and re-arranged the blanket to give Lady Aisllyn a little more modesty. Kahlahnni moved to her normal assigned position in the room, where she had spent most of the last five years when not in her own room, and waited.

There was a polite tap on the door and with no Lady Aisllyn to speak, Lahnni held tight to her courage and spoke louder than she had in years. "Enter."

The door opened and the housekeeper entered. Lahnni dropped her eyes, but cleared her throat and spoke before the housekeeper could say anything. "I believe Lady Aisllyn has passed."

Lahnni kept her eyes down but heard the rushing of feet toward the bed. Silence filled the room for several moments as the housekeeper watched her mistress. Eventually, she spoke, "I need to inform a few people. Stay with her."

"Yes, Ma'am."

"I know Lady Aisllyn allowed you to sit when it was just the two of you. You may sit today; it will be a long day and I don't want her left alone. Do you understand?"

"Yes, Ma'am."

The housekeeper bustled out of the room and with no one to see her, Kahlahnni flopped down in the high-backed chair that had been assigned to her and let her tears flow. It was only then did Kahlahnni wonder what would happen to her now she had no Lady Aisllyn to take care of.

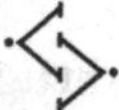

An uneasy feeling settled in the pit of her stomach as she took in the middle-aged man sitting behind the desk. There was nothing outwardly interesting about him. He looked like every other male she had ever met; tall, blondish hair with blue eyes, and an air of arrogance cloaked him. His wide shoulders and barrel chest made her feel even smaller than normal and she tried to shrink herself down to invisible.

"Come, sit," he ordered as she stood in the doorway to the office he used since he had arrived at the Manor house the week prior.

Kahlahnni didn't want to enter the room, but she had no choice. Technically, as a servant to Lady Aisllyn, her nephew, the Lord of Burrop, was now Lahnni's new owner until she was branded at the age of nineteen and her true self was revealed. She could of course be sold or given away before that time if he chose. She did what she was told and stepped into the cold, bare room with its hard chairs and large black lacquered desk. Lahnni couldn't bring herself to sit, her flight instinct was strong. So, instead, she stood behind the chair as if it was a shield.

"You served my aunt as her personal maid."

She didn't know if it was a question or statement, so remained quiet and kept her eyes lowered in the hope he wouldn't notice their color.

"I am told my aunt liked you but no one knows what to do with you now." He shuffled a few papers on the desk before he pushed his chair back and stood and walked slowly around his desk.

Kahlahnni was glad she had chosen to remain standing; as it was, she was small compared to his hulking frame, but she couldn't imagine how she would feel if she were sitting. Her feelings of uneasiness grew as he moved toward her. This was not a good man, and for the first time in five years she had that skin-crawling feeling just like when Ambrosse was around and had cornered her.

"Remove that cap," he ordered.

"My Lord?"

"I want to see your hair."

Fear made her stomach clench as she lifted a shaking hand to remove the cap she wore to cover her despised hair. It had taken so long for it to grow back after Ambrosse had hacked it off and she was secretly proud of how silky and shiny it looked in the moonlight when she was by herself. She prayed it didn't offend him the way it seemed to bother everyone else. The soft curls fell around her shoulders and she clutched the white cap to her chest as she waited for his response.

Lahnni held her breath as the Lord of Burrop walked behind her. She almost squealed with fright as she felt his hand brush her shoulder and lift a lock of her hair. *Please don't let him cut it, please don't let him cut it*, she chanted in her mind.

"Beautiful," he spoke quietly. "Why do you wear the cap?" he asked as he dropped her hair and moved around to the front of the desk, which he lent on. She was grateful to have the chair between them.

"To keep it off my face," she lied.

"You could tie it back as everyone else does."

She didn't know what to say, so kept quiet.

"Look at me," he said with less authority in his voice than he had when he ordered her to remove the head covering.

This, for no reason she could fathom, made her feel anxious. She did what she was told and slowly raised her eyes to meet his. She didn't like what she saw when he looked at her and she clenched her fists to keep still and her emotions under control.

"What do I do with you?" He smiled at her, but it wasn't friendly. He stood up from where he had been reclining on the edge of the desk and reached out and touched her face, running his hand along her jawline.

She felt violently ill and a clear picture formed in her mind. Lahnni began to tremble as what she saw registered. She was tied to a four-poster bed, spread eagle and naked. Hovering over her was the Lord of Burrop, naked and holding a cane. Thin red welts covered her thighs and stomach, where he had obviously already used the cane. Behind him hovered a long line of young blonde girls, bound and gagged, and covered in welts, all with their throats slit. The scene was horrifying and it took all of Lahnni's efforts not to dry retch. On the other side of the bed stood an obese blonde woman, who glared at the lord, clear hatred on her face while she wielded a blood-covered knife.

Kahlahnni fought for air as she felt like she was being pulled further into the vision. With no regard for the consequences, she pulled her face away from the caressing hand and broke the skin on skin contact. The vision faded and she blinked rapidly in the hope of clearing it completely from her mind, and just like the last time she felt threatened by Ambrosse, she lifted her head in defiance and stared at the lord rather than cower in fear. Blurred images of pretty blondes with cut throats lingered a little longer and she concentrated on a spot in the middle of his forehead rather than look him in the eye. She felt tainted by his touch as if she would never be clean again.

"The fun I could have with you." He leered at her.

Lahnni held her ground and fought the urge to recoil at his words. She didn't know if what she had seen was true, but this man gave her a strong feeling that it was. It was only then did she realize that she had a tight grip on the back of the chair as if it was the only thing keeping her standing.

Before anything more could be said, heavy footsteps filled the hall and the lord moved to sit behind his desk. Lahnni concentrated on keeping her breathing even and reminded herself that the vision wasn't real, it was all in her head. What she had seen was sickening, but not confirmed. All she knew was that she needed to get as far away from this man as she could. But how?

There was a polite knock on the open door and Kahlahnni removed her hands from the back of the chair and reverted to her usual posture of hunched shoulders and eyes cast downward. Belatedly, she realized that her hair was still exposed, the cap now lay at her feet, obviously dropped when Lord Channing had touched her.

"Yes?" the Lord answered the polite knock.

His steward, who had arrived with the Lord of Burrop, spoke in his nasal tones. "My Lord, a Captain Emmettin Finnley would like a few words."

"Of course," Lord Channing said magnanimously. "Please, Captain, come and sit. Tea, coffee, or something a little more bracing?"

"Thank you, but no. I have other matters to attend to."

Lahnni didn't know what to do. She had not been dismissed and didn't know if she should curtsy and leave or wait for someone to tell her to go. Should she move to the corner and serve them when required as she had for her former mistress? She had felt lost since Lady Aisllyn had passed, confused by what she should be doing. The last few weeks had been dreadful as no one spoke to her to tell her what to do, and when she had attempted to ask she had been ignored or told to wait in her room and not bother anyone until the Lord arrived and assigned her a new role.

"Very well, Captain, what can I help you with?"

Lahnni took a step backward as the newcomer moved closer to the chair. She longed to look up and see this man. She didn't know how to describe it other than he felt safe. She typically only felt bad emotions, warnings as such. This was new. Kahlahnni decided that unless she was dismissed she was going to stay and find out why he had come.

"I have come for the girl."

"I beg your pardon?" Lord Channing sounded mildly surprised. It was hard to tell without looking at his face.

"Lady Aisllyn gifted her to me upon her death and I have come to collect what is rightfully mine."

Kahlahnni was confused. This man had never been to visit Lady Aisllyn in the five years Lahnni had served her. Why was he lying and what girl did he speak of?

"To my knowledge, there is no such arrangement in place." Lord Channing's voice was non-committal.

She didn't know who to believe.

"Kahlahnni, I am here to take you with me. You should go and pack, as we will be leaving here immediately." The highly polished shoes and dark gray pant leg of the one Lord Channing called Captain stepped closer to her. She was so startled by his words that she forgot her fear and looked up.

Lahnni didn't know how to feel about being handed over to someone and being seen as no more valuable than a good working horse, but she knew she would rather take her chances with this newcomer than stay with the lord and find out if her vision of the beaten women were true. "I have nothing to take with me." Her voice was quiet and sad.

The Captain frowned before smiling kindly. His bright blue eyes crinkled in the corners and she noticed he had freckles across his pale skin. The uniform he wore was all gray but had round, shiny gold buttons spaced evenly down the front of the jacket and in a row of three at the edge of each sleeve. There were flaps on the shoulders where a braid of gold cord was held in place. On the upper part of each sleeve were patches with different patterns—she didn't know what they meant but they looked impressive. She watched his eyes roam over her, taking in her dark hair, eyes, and richer skin tone. But unlike most she met, he didn't sneer, nor shy away, he just continued to smile kindly.

"Well, if she has nothing to pack, we should be on our way."

"Hang on. I have seen no evidence of this agreement. You can't just sweep in here and announce you are taking my servant." Lord Channing rose from his seat.

The man in uniform turned from Lahnni and faced the lord. "I can and I will." His voice was filled with authority.

"I am Lord of Burrop. I am the second chair in the Council of Jaggiron and hold sway in the court of King Tommofey," the heavy-chested man boasted. "Unless you can produce a document to prove your claim I will bid you good day."

"I am willing to stand before any court you choose and swear under oath that what I speak is true. Who will they believe, I wonder? A decorated captain of the last war or a man of your proclivities who wields less power than he thinks he does?"

"My proclivities?" Lord Channing's carefully crafted nonchalance appeared to slip as his voice rose an octave.

"Do you really want this known? Do you wish to raise their ire if they discover you kept her when you had no right?" The captain leaned across the desk and his voice dropped to a whisper. "Is she worth it?"

Kahlahnni wished she knew what they were talking about. So much of it was confusing.

The Lord of Burrop paled and sank slowly back in his chair. "Yes, I think this one could be more trouble than what she is worth." He looked from the captain to

Kahlahnni. "I have no desire to anger her people." He paused as if coming to a conclusion. "Yes, I agree to dismiss her from my services and sign her to yours." He studied her for a few moments longer and Kahlahnni did not shy away from his stare, if anything she held her head a little higher. But as she stood defiant, the relief she should have felt did not come; instead, all she wanted to know was who was "her people"?

Chapter 3

The sound of excited voices reached Kahlahnni and her heart lurched for a moment. A feeling of foreboding had been growing within her for the past two days. It had started when the town mayor had received word that the priest that would be performing the branding ceremony this year would arrive within the next few days. Expertly, Lahnni put the hot, flat metal iron on the red coals and folded the shirt she had been pressing, ready for it to be picked up later that afternoon. She quietly moved toward the open shutters, but was careful to remain hidden from anyone who might pass by the house. She didn't need anyone tattling that she was shirking her work. Jossiner, the man who owned the laundry in which she worked, left her alone to do her duties now that she had proven herself, but she had been whipped twice when people had complained that their clothing had not been ready on time. Both instances had been the fault of Lahnni's immediate superior, Marggot, who had agreed to have items ready in impossible time frames, but Lahnni had born the brunt of the punishment.

The babbling voices rose and Lahnni could make out snippets of sentences.

"They will be here in about an hour."

"It's a different priest from last year."

"Is the Inn ready for them?"

"Are the supplicants gathering?"

Lahnni frowned at that last statement. Where were they supposed to be gathering? No one had told her they were required somewhere. She felt sick as her internal tension grew. The process of branding was an ordeal in itself, but for someone like herself, who didn't fit in or didn't instinctively know her caste, it was worse. This would be an irrevocable moment that would determine the remainder of her life. Once branded, you were left with that label until the day you died and there was no changing it. Ever.

A door slammed, and Kahlahnni jumped with fright. Moving quickly she put on her protective glove and picked up the flat iron, rushing to spread out a rose-colored skirt in a soft linen material. As she pressed the iron to the skirt, the door swung open and in walked Marggot carrying a basket of laundered items ready for pressing. Lahnni wanted to groan at the sight, but instead kept her head lowered and her eyes focused.

"Are you still here?" the raspy voice of Marggot snarled at her.

It wasn't often that the woman spoke directly to her. They worked in silence most of the time, as Lahnni did not need to be trained or guided. "I didn't know I wasn't supposed to be here." She tried to sound meek.

Before more could be said, there was a loud knock on the door of the shop. Marggot rushed to answer while Lahnni returned the iron to the coals and went to get her large straw hat. She didn't know where she had to be but was happy to be anywhere but here.

"I am here to get Lahnni," a young girl's voice announced with the exuberance of a nine-year-old.

Relief washed over Lahnni as she shoved the hat on and made for the door, keeping her eyes down as she moved past Marggot and out into the hot day.

"Papa says you have to come quick," Margueritte said impatiently, her cute button nose wrinkling as she tried to look stern.

The young girl was almost as tall as the shorter than average Lahnni, even though there was almost a decade difference in age, and kept up as Kahlahnni set out for their home. They didn't speak. Kahlahnni had stopped speaking to Margueritte in public—unless absolutely necessary—almost immediately after she had been brought to live with them. Lahnni had come upon several children teasing Margueritte for having the 'odd girl' living with them. The child had been bravely trying not to cry and attempting to explain that Kahlahnni was just like everyone else. No one wanted to know.

Kahlahnni had rescued her from the teasing children and on the way home had decided to keep her distance from the three girls she lived with for their safety. In their home, they spoke freely, but outside Lahnni walked in front or behind and never spoke to them in the hope that people would forget where she lived. It worked most of the time.

Today was different. Her emotions were building. She didn't know what was to come and it was making her anxious. Margueritte kept pace by running, but Lahnni didn't slow her slightly wider, rushed strides; something was coming and she felt the need to run towards it.

It didn't take them long to reach the baker's shop that they lived behind, and the girls hurried through a side gate and into the huge hot kitchen, where all the bread and other pastries were made each morning. The kitchen had been scrubbed and a delicious smelling stew now cooked slowly in the coals of the one oven that still remained lit. As Lahnni stepped through the door and found Emmettin sitting there in his uniform, which he rarely wore, she felt an easing of her confusion. The captain would tell her what was happening.

"Thank you, Margueritte. You can go help your mother." He spoke kindly to his eldest daughter, but it was clear she was not allowed to stay.

Margueritte didn't argue, it was not in her nature; instead, she walked through the kitchen and opened another door that led to the bakery that the family owned. Cellecia's voice could be heard through the open door. "Did you get Lahnni?"

"Yes, Mamma," Margueritte answered as she pulled the door closed behind her.

Kahlahnni removed her hat and hung it on a hook in the corner. Emmettin didn't wait for her to sit or ask what was happening. "You must hurry, my girl, the supplicants are expected at the Barrel of Fish Inn in half a turning. They neglected to tell us the details of the summons until the last minute."

He didn't need to tell her who "they" were. They were the people of the town who made her life miserable any chance they could, for the simple reason that she looked different from them.

Emmettin went on. "They couldn't not tell you about the meeting, as it is their responsibility to notify all supplicants, but I think they hoped if they put it off long enough then you would arrive late." He ran his hand over his graying hair and rolled his blue eyes, showing his frustration. "The pettiness of these people never ceases to amaze me. Hurry and wash your face, tidy your hair, and change your apron. You represent our family today, and I want you to stand tall. You have nothing to fear from the priest and his troops. They are simply here to do their job and move onto the next town. I will walk you to the Barrel myself."

Lahnni ran to the room she shared with Margueritte and the next youngest child, Mechelle, and found a blood red apron already laid out on her bed. Cellecia was always telling her that she looked beautiful in red and had obviously decided that that was what Lahnni should wear. Grateful to be guided, Lahnni took off the sky blue apron she wore over the navy cotton dress she had put on this morning and hurried to wash her face in the clean water basin that had been left for her on the small sideboard that the girls had in their room. Cellecia, as usual, had thought of everything to save time and help where she could.

After washing her face and putting on the pretty red apron, Kahlahnni tackled her thick, long, dark hair. She unpinned it from the bun she typically wore, so most of it was hidden under the sun hat she wore outside and it flowed down her back. Quickly she ran a comb through it and with practiced ease she braided it into a single long plait down her back, securing it with a pretty red ribbon. Lahnni returned to the kitchen to find Emmettin buttoning up his Captain's uniform jacket—the relief Lahnni felt to see that gray jacket was almost palpable. The townsfolk always averted their eyes and left her alone when Emmettin reminded everyone exactly who he was and that she, in essence, belonged to him until the branding ceremony determined her fate. And with the thoughts of the ceremony and it's unknown outcome her anxiety returned and her fear grew.

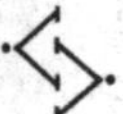

"I am here to allay some of your fears. To answer your questions and assure you that whatever you are feeling is very normal. In my time in the guard, I have seen large men faint and frail girls not flinch. We are all different, and whatever your reaction is you shouldn't be ashamed of it."

Kahlahnni sat in the main room of the town's only inn with five other supplicants for this year's branding ceremony. The inn had been closed to its usual clientele while the meeting was held. This year's supplicants were made up of four girls and two boys and what they had in common is that they would all turn nineteen in the same year. Several of the young women and one of the young men Lahnni had not seen before and assumed that they were from the sprawling farming lands that surrounded the town of Gennestenmont on the left-hand side. The boy she did know from the town had always simply ignored her, neither engaging in the nasty remarks towards her nor stopping them when he was near enough to overhear them. He had arrived at the meeting with his head cleanly shaven but for a short topknot indicating to everyone that he hoped the branding to come would reveal his calling to the Brothers of Jaggir. Lahnni didn't know much about the different religious groups of Segarris. Cellecia and Emmettin told her that none were to be truly trusted as they all put their own needs before the Gods they pretended to serve, and that being so far away from the major cities there was no need to know more. The one supplicant she did know was the inn keeper's daughter, Traiss, and she had come down the stairs to the side of the large common room once everyone else was assembled, as if they had all been awaiting her appearance. She wore a dress of the softest lemon and a stiff white apron that had too many frills to make it practical. Her blonde hair had been curled and pinned in a messy pile on the top of her head and her cheeks and lips rouged. Kahlahnni had looked back to where she had been staring at a black scorch mark on the cold stone floor once the overly costumed young woman had reached the bottom of the stairway, and secretly wished she had the confidence to enter a room and have everyone stare at her like that.

"I am not going to lie, it is going to hurt...a lot." His words caught her attention.

His voice was calm. He sounded like he cared and Lahnni was shocked to find herself raising her eyes to look at him. Her eyes moved up from his shiny black riding boots, over his black soldier's uniform with its red and yellow trim, and looked upon his face. She was surprised to see a kind face, almost plain, with its lightly tanned skin and a spattering of freckles across his nose. A clean-shaven chin and generous lips matched his light eyebrows and already lined forehead, though he couldn't have been more than twenty-five. What Lahnni found mesmerizing were his eyes. They were startling in their intensity. Large and almond-shaped, framed by thick lashes he had aquamarine eyes, the color she had always imagined the ocean was. He caught her staring and smiled at her reassuringly before moving on to smile at the person in front of her.

Kahlahnni was astounded. He was a stranger, someone she had had no interaction with, but he did not recoil at her appearance, look disgusted, nor sneer as if she were something lesser. His eyes swept back to her as he went on to explain the ceremony and what they were to expect. She could not describe how she was feeling at that moment; it was a completely new experience. Then he spoke and she was too focused on his words to consider why he had not recoiled at her looks like the three outliers had done when she had made her way to the chair in the back. They had all stopped to stare at her with openly hostile looks.

"You will be expected to arrive here a half turning before dawn tomorrow. You may break your fast before the ceremony if you wish. Anyone in the town or surrounding areas is welcome to bear witness." He paused and something about the next words made Kahlahnni's uneasiness intensify. "The outcome of each branding will be final. No matter what you think you are or should be, what the branding reveals of your true self is what you will become and remain. The law will always be enforced. The caste system was designed to protect all of Segarris' people and make certain the nation thrived." He looked at each of them in turn, his beautiful eyes coming to Lahnni last. "Does anyone have any questions?"

Lahnni dropped her gaze to the ground as his stare made her feel strange things. Something odd stirred within her and she had no name for it. She felt like she would burst from her skin with everything she was feeling and sensing at the moment; it was a difficult situation and it was moments like these that she wished she had someone to confide in. To help her understand what was happening to her. She knew there was something different about her and it wasn't just her appearance, but she was too scared to tell anyone what she felt or saw sometimes when she was around or had skin on skin contact with someone. She had concluded long ago that it wasn't normal and she didn't need the only people in her life who treated her normally to stop treating her that way if they found out how strange she was.

Instead of sitting in this room, she wished she could escape to her favorite hiding place in the miller's barn, where she was far enough away from anyone that no emotions reached her and she didn't live in fear of touching anyone and accidentally seeing something she didn't want to see.

"I have a question," the inn keeper's daughter, Traiss, piped up.

"Go ahead." The kind eyed man turned from Kahlahnni. "What do you want to know?"

"Have you ever had the brand reveal a secret identity?"

"You mean like someone with royal blood who didn't know they were?"

"Yes." Traiss's voice went up an octave with excitement.

"No." Her face fell and he smiled at her. "That has happened, but it is rare and hasn't occurred in the last hundred years or so. Most people in the ruling castes do not go into hiding and birth children in secret."

"Oh, okay."

Kahlahnni wondered if the inn keeper's daughter fancied herself to be a princess in hiding. A completely ludicrous idea, but who knew what went on in people's heads.

"Any other questions?"

Everyone shook their heads, and Lahnni found herself joining in. It was an odd thing to be part of a group of peers and to have her voice be relevant. She knew that they would all still have more questions, but no one was comfortable enough to express them in front of the soldiers or other young people as they didn't want to be judged for being nervous or asking stupid things.

"Very well, you are dismissed. I will see you all tomorrow morning." He nodded his head and walked away from the assembled supplicants and to a priest with a shaved head but full beard, indicating that he was a Brother of the Order of Seggar, who sat reading a heavy book at a table in the far corner of the common room.

While everyone stood and stretched their muscles and made a few friendly comments to each other, Kahlahnni sat silently and waited for them all to move away. She had once again returned to her default setting of shoulders hunched, head and eyes cast downwards. As they shuffled out of the room, Lahnni finally stood. She didn't stretch even though she wanted to, in case it brought attention to herself, and silently made her way toward the side door they had entered by. Everyone had left and she was the only supplicant still in the room. Lahnni moved to open the door when an arm blocked her and a tall body leaned on the door frame, subtly blocking her exit. "Hello, Creeper."

Her body trembled and she fought the vision that wanted to engulf her. Lahnni had spent years reliving that nightmare and she didn't want to be drawn back into it. She stood still, fighting for control and hoping that the man blocking her way out was not Ambrosse. Slowly she raised her head to look full in the face of her childhood tormentor. The boy that had deliberately and cruelly stalked her, cut her hair, stole her food, and broke her thumb. His smile was just as she remembered. Cold and disturbing. There was no warmth in his pale eyes. The boy was now a man, powerfully built and honed to kill in the King's army. It was a terrifying thought. He bent down to whisper in her ear and she took several steps backward. He chuckled quietly. "When will you learn you can't escape me, Creeper?" he whispered.

Lahnni blinked at him, not understanding what he meant.

"You will be branded tomorrow and the world will see what I already know. You will carry the mark of a servant and I will buy you to do with what I wish. Today will be the last day you defy me." He raised his hand to touch her face and she took another step back, out of his reach. "Enjoy your freedom." He grasped the handle and opened the door for her to find Cellecia waiting on the other side. Ambrosse and Cellecia stared at each other as Lahnni rushed outside, but before he could close the door her vision overtook her and she stopped in the doorway, blocking it.

Images filled her mind. Fire, Ambrosse falling, his mouth wide with terror, wooden planks and blood, and Kahlahnni standing in the center of it all. Instinct kicked in and she reached out and grasped the front of his shirt before he had a chance to react, she pulled him down so they were face to face. "Continue on the path you have chosen and you will die a horrible death. Leave me alone." Their noses were almost touching. "You have been warned," she hissed at him before shoving him away and running to Cellecia.

"Are you all right?" The woman who had always made certain Lahnni was cared for asked as they headed toward home. "What was that all about?"

Lahnni wanted to blurt out about the pictures that still lingered in her mind, but hesitated; even though Cellecia had done so much for Lahnni there was still a barrier. Lahnni still didn't fit properly, she knew deep down she was different, and telling Cellecia would make that difference more noticeable. The way she lived now wasn't ideal with all the hostility toward her from the townspeople, she couldn't risk Cellecia and Emmettin turning her out because they thought there was something wrong with her due to the visions she had.

"As long as you know you can tell me anything," Cellecia pressed her.

"Ambrosse said that I will be branded a servant. Do you think I will?" Lahnni asked. She left out the threat to own her.

"Personally, I don't think so."

"What will happen to me if I am a servant?" she pushed.

Cellecia stopped in the middle of the main street they walked down and looked at her, her face stern. "Nothing will change if you are branded with the servant symbol. Technically Emmettin owns you as you were gifted to him by Lady Aisllyn as far as everyone knows. Tomorrow you will either be a free person because your brand will say you are or you will remain a servant and he will remain your master. You will remain with the family until you die or wish to be purchased by someone you choose."

They began to walk again and relief filled Lahnni, pushing the horrid visions of Ambrosse dying away. "Ambrosse said he would buy me tomorrow when my brand shows everyone that I am a servant."

"Over my dead body," muttered Cellecia.

It *will actually be over his dead body*, Lahnni thought to herself but didn't voice it.

Chapter 4

The night had cooled considerably and as everyone gathered around the fire that the sacred brand was resting in, Kahlahnni tried to keep her emotions under control while she stood in between Cellecia and Emmettin, who had worn his uniform for the occasion. It was almost unbearable standing with the other supplicants, so she had distanced herself slightly. Strangely, she thought it was as if all their emotions were emanating onto her. Her own trepidation and fear were difficult enough without dealing with five other people. The sooner this was over the better. She was looking forward to her life returning to normal now she had been reassured by Cellecia that even if she was branded a servant rather than a commoner she would be safe and able to continue to live with them. Lahnni didn't want to think about if she was branded to become a priestess; she knew barely anything about the male orders and nothing about the female ones.

Fluffy white clouds drifted slowly across the sky, in no hurry to be anywhere, which felt in complete contrast to Lahnni's current sense of urgency. The sun rose behind the huge mountains to the right of the town, throwing off beautiful hues of pink and red. Someone hit a kettle drum, gaining everyone's attention, and the gathered townspeople fell silent.

The ceremony would take place in the center of the town square, where all major events were held. The inn doors swung open and two soldiers stepped out before the priest with his full reddish-blond beard and bald head walked through. His inky black ceremonial robes made him appear sinister in the false dawn light. Ambrosse and another soldier came out behind the priest, they both carried lit torches to help him see by, she assumed. Then another pair of soldiers stepped out, carrying a small metal chest between them. The man who had spoken to them yesterday was the last to exit and Lahnni noted that he nodded to someone out of her line of sight. She curiously looked around to discover that there were several more soldiers stationed around the crowd. She wondered how often there was trouble at these ceremonies. All the soldiers were pale in skin tone, but their hair colors varied to a mid-brown that she had never seen before. It was astounding to see something other than blonde and reddish hues. They still didn't look like her, but they also all didn't look the same.

Lahnni was grateful for the slowly disappearing darkness as it gave her the chance to watch what was happening and keep a lookout for Ambrosse. She knew what he was capable of and had seen the joy her fear had brought him when he had stopped her from leaving yesterday. He had not changed and now he was far bigger and stronger and she would have no way of stopping him if he chose to hunt her down and torture her. She didn't know the rules of the army and if they frowned upon it or thought it acceptable, but she figured the latter as that had been what his branding had revealed him to belong to when it had been his time. Why would the branding, the divine power of the Gods, put him in the army if that was not his place?

There was much she didn't know about the branding, and every time she had broached the subject with Cellecia or Emmettin they had become evasive, and other than some fairly basic things the rest was brushed over with "we must not taint the ceremony." She had caught them on several occasions sharing a look of concern when they thought she wasn't looking. Was it true that she couldn't know what was going on, or were they hiding something? Those secret looks bothered her greatly.

What she did know was that there were five brand symbols that she had seen on people's wrists her entire life. Cellecia had the Commoner brand, a single vertical line with a short line across each end. On one side of the vertical line were two dots, along the other side were two diagonal lines. Most people that lived in the town had this symbol.

Several of the people that had worked in the kitchen of Lady Aislynn carried the scorched marking of the Bond-slave brand. It was similar to the Commoner brand with a single vertical line and a short line across each end. On each side of the vertical line were two diagonal lines and it had a dot at the bottom of the long vertical line. Lahnni had been quietly praying that she wouldn't receive the Servant brand, even though Emmettin had bought her from Lord Channing four years ago, implying she was nothing more than a servant. And now after Ambrosse's threat, it was even more vital. She needed that Commoner brand, she needed to be free to make her own choices.

Captain Finnley carried the Warrior brand with pride upon his left wrist. It had a V shape with a horizontal line across the bottom and a dot in the center. All of the lines had shorter lines on their ends. It was similar to the Religion Brand. The Religion brand was inverted and had a line at the base of its V, creating a triangle, there was also an added dot at the base. Kahlahnni had commented that the brands were markedly similar and Emmettin had explained that all brands were paired as far as he knew. The Warrior and Religion matched because they were both protectors of the people. One for the body and one for the soul.

Lahnni had considered that, and in a moment of clarity, she understood that the Commoner and Servant brands looked similar too, which made sense that the two lowest castes for the population would match. She had then re-called the brand on Lady Aisllyn's wrist and how that had been different from any other she had seen. Lady Aisllyn had been noble, a far distant relative of a long-dead king. The brand had been a single vertical line, with the short lines at each end. At the center of the long line was a dot on each side, and above the dot on the right was a horizontal line and a diagonal line meeting at the vertical line, this was repeated on the left-hand side below the dot. Kahlahnni had known better than to ask but she had often wondered, once she had discovered that all brands were pairs, what the matching Royal brand looked like and who wore it.

The ringing of the kettle drum intruded on her thoughts and she was brought back to the present. The sky had lightened considerably while she had been focused on her hopes of being heard by the Gods to not be branded a servant. The crowd was restless and the uneasy sensation continued to grow inside her as well as be thrust upon her by the other supplicants. She wished she understood what was happening to her at these moments and had some way of controlling it. She pushed the thoughts away, like she always did, determined not to dwell on something that frightened her when she pondered it for too long. Why couldn't she just be the same as everyone else? She was different in every way and it was tiring to fight against it all of the time.

The drums stopped and it felt like everyone held their breath. "It is time," the Priest for the Order of Seggar told the assembled crowd.

"Go stand with the rest," Cellecia told her quietly. She did what she was instructed.

"Will the supplicant come willingly?" He looked to the group of young people to his right, his eyes falling on the boy with the shaved head, save for the top knot.

The young man who obviously hoped to join the Brothers of Jaggir by gaining the Religious branding stepped forward. "I am," he announced. He had rolled up his left sleeve in anticipation of what was to come. He sat on the three-legged wooden stool and placed his arm on the old wooden table that had been brought from the inn, palm up.

Someone started a slow beat on the drum and the priest began to walk clockwise around the large bonfire that had been built in the center of the market square, he muttered softly, but Lahnni could not understand the words. After making three circuits of the bright fire, the bearded priest stopped and faced the flames, he threw his hands into the air and released some form of powder. The orange flames doubled in size and turned a bright green and the priest picked up the rod that had been sitting between two rocks since Lahnni had arrived. The end of the rod was the same colored fluorescent green as the flames and looked to be a solid disc shape. Kahlahnni was fascinated. How was it going to make different patterns on the skin?

Two soldiers stepped forward, one put both his hands on the shoulders of the supplicant while the other soldier held his hand and upper forearm down firmly on the table. The priest in his flowing black robes and long tasseled belt continued to murmur as he held the rod aloft and with great care brought it carefully down on the exposed inner wrist. The supplicant grunted once, but otherwise held still as the skin could be heard to sizzle for a few moments before the priest removed the brand to reveal the religious symbol. "Let it be recorded that the supplicant has been given the honor of joining the ranks of the Priesthood. I welcome him in their stead." The assembled crowd sighed with relief and the branding rod was placed back in the fire and the priest again began to circle the fire that had returned to the normal color of reds and oranges.

Lahnni continued to watch the supplicant as a wet cloth was placed over his raw burn and more words of congratulations were uttered as he was led to the other side of the fire, now an official member of the adults of Segarris. Even now, Kahlahnni knew that no matter what brand she received it would not result in her being welcomed by the people in this town; she would still be the strange, short girl with dark hair and eyes. It made her sad, but not as it once did. When she had come to live with Cellecia, Emmettin, and their children in the middle of the large town rather than being isolated in the Boarding house or the Manor house, Lahnni had thought she might have more chance of being accepted as there would be more different people, but that wasn't the case and the townspeople had shunned her just as quickly and vehemently as everyone else had. Most simply ignored her, but some went out of their way to be cruel or snide while a few, usually young people in a group, occasionally attempted to physically harm her by shoving past her, tripping her when carrying something, and on rare occasions, she had been pinched from behind while in a crowd.

The priest finished his three circuits of the fire and again raised his hand quickly, throwing the powder and turning the flames iridescent green. He nodded to one of the farm girls that had come into the town for the ceremony and she meekly stepped forward. Lahnni noted her eyes glistened in the early morning light and she guessed they were from unshed tears. The soldier who had spoken to them yesterday moved to her and took her elbow, gently leading her to the chair, and he appeared to be speaking to her. Kahlahnni was so intent on watching him and his calm demeanor amongst all the trepidation and fear from the supplicants, and the expectation and anticipation from the crowd that she missed the priest raise the brand and move toward the now visibly sobbing girl. The two soldiers that had held the male supplicant seemed to have a firmer grip on the girl and the kind voiced soldier now stood next to her, allowing the girl to grasp his hand tightly. The priest lowered the glowing green brand and the girl cried out, but wisely sat still. It was over in moments but her sobbing continued as the priest returned to his circling and preparing for the next supplicant and she was led to the other side where her awaiting family comforted her and congratulated her on being branded a Commoner.

Lahnni continued to focus on keeping calm and out of the reach of anyone as her heightened emotions coupled with theirs would almost be guaranteed to bring on clearer visions that she might not wish to see. The next two supplicants were the other outlier farm girl who joined the ranks of Commoners, while the male was revealed to have the Warrior symbol. Neither was overly distraught with the branding. The farm girl gasped loudly but there were no tears, and the young man sat stoically, looking straight ahead into the embers of the green fire.

As the priest walked his circuit of the now red fire, Lahnni knew with certainty that the inn keeper's daughter would be chosen next. Traiss had on a pretty pink dress with a paler pink apron over the top. The sleeves were quarter length so she didn't have to mar the appearance of the outfit by rolling them up or getting them soiled with the wet cloth or blood after the branding.

"Creeper," a voice spoke quietly behind her, making Lahnni jump with fright and take a step away from Ambrosse, who had snuck up on her while she was concentrating on the ceremony.

Accidentally Lahnni brushed her hand against Traiss's bare arm and a vision of the blonde girl standing in front of a throne came to her. She was dressed in an elaborately jeweled dress which looked incredibly heavy and uncomfortable and carried a haughty look on her pinched features. Lahnni suspected that Traiss was hoping to be exposed as a missing noble and that she would be whisked away to live in luxury and own servants rather than work in her father's inn until she married. For the first time, Lahnni took a breath, and instead of pulling away from the contact she deliberately kept the touch light and allowed her thoughts to focus on what she was seeing. In her mind, Lahnni spoke softly as if to another person, 'Is she royal?" The vision changed slightly and now the inn keeper's daughter stood before the throne holding a golden crown aloft. The crown shone brightly in the sunlight streaming into the room until the sky darkened and the room turned gloomy. The golden crown began to crumble in the girl's hands and while she desperately tried to hold onto it it was to no avail the crown turned to dust and blew away with a wind that filled the room.

"Creeper, you can't hide from me."

The vision shattered with the sound of Ambrosse's voice and Lahnni felt her anger rise. "Leave me alone," she hissed at him. She again took another step away from him, he smirked and moved to close the gap again when a large body came between them.

"Is there an issue?" Emmettin asked.

Ambrosse saluted sharply, recognizing the seniority of the Captain's uniform. "No, Sir. I was just becoming reacquainted with an old friend."

Emmettin looked Ambrosse up and down with clear disdain. "I am well aware of who you are and how you know Kahlahnni. Stay away from my property."

They were all distracted from any further discussion by the sudden outburst of hysterical crying as it was revealed that Traiss was to spend the rest of her life branded as a Commoner. Lahnni would have found the situation ridiculous if she now wasn't so focused on the fact that it was her turn.

As she watched the priest put the branding iron back in the orange flames and started his muttering and walking, she decided that whatever was going to happen she was not going to cower or whimper, she was going to face it head-on. She had a feeling that most of the crowd had come for this moment, to see the girl they couldn't break with their jibes and exclusion finally be revealed for what they all thought she should be...a petty lowest-ranked Servant. Born to serve others with no hope of owning anything or making her own decisions. Although they had rights and were protected from being overworked or abused they would always rely on others' goodwill and better nature to survive in this world.

Lahnni walked over to the stool and sat down without being invited by the priest. She rolled up her sleeve to reveal her left wrist and laid her arm across the table in anticipation. A murmur ran through the crowd at her audacity, but she was beyond caring. Let the brand reveal her to be the servant they all thought she deserved to be. She would endure, just as she had always done. Emmettin and Cellecia had promised her that she would be safe, so her fear of the Servant brand had eased. She just wanted it over with.

The priest completed his final circle of the fire and threw the powder to make the flames green and only when he had retrieved the glowing green brand and turned did he realize she was already seated. He frowned but didn't halt his quiet chanting as he moved toward her.

The soldier behind her placed his hands on her shoulders and she was grateful for the material of her dress underneath his hands. She watched the soldier move to take her hand and upper forearm and braced herself for the vision that would surely come. With this much heightened emotion swirling within her it was inevitable.

As his hands closed on her, Lahnni's mind filled with images of a young girl, no more than five, running and laughing through a sunflower filled meadow. She had strawberry blonde hair and sparkling cornflower blue eyes, the soldier was chasing her, his face joyous and happy. He scooped up the little girl and tossed her into the air, making her squeal with laughter. It was the most beautiful moment Kahlahnni had ever experienced. The sheer love for that child and the happiness that carefree moment brought to both of them.

A scream ripped from her throat as the brand pressed into her skin. The image shattered and was replaced by the feeling of determination mingled with frustration that seemed to be coming from the priest. Lahnni was confused; what had happened to make him feel that way? He had seemed so calm before, almost arrogant in his abilities to perform the ceremony with little fuss.

Pain tore up her arm and through her body, engulfing her entire being. Why was it so very painful for her? The crowd had gone quiet and the only sound was her screams and the priest's louder chanting. After what seemed an eternity and like she would never regain her senses, the brand was removed and those closest to her became enraged. She looked down to see what her brand was to discover that her skin held no marking. Not a single burn marred her olive-toned skin. How was it possible?

"Hold her," the priest ordered as he put the branding rod back in the fire and stalked over to the small metal chest that had been carried out earlier.

Kahlahnni tried to calm her nerves. Something was wrong with the brand and that had been the issue. The priest would rectify the situation and they would resume the ceremony quickly. She sought out the familiar faces of Emmettin and Cellecia for comfort, only to find them both with worried looks upon their faces. Did they know something she didn't?

The silence of the crowd disappeared and was replaced with the growing murmuring of dissent. Through the overwhelming emotions that were rolling from the townspeople toward her, she could hear snippets of conversation.

"I told you there was something wrong with her."

"I always knew she was trouble."

"Is there really no brand?"

"What did you think was going to happen? She is one of them."

That caught Lahnni's attention and she wanted to know what "them" meant. Did everyone know why she looked different but no one had bothered to tell her? Was it possible that there was a reason she was not like everyone else? Why had Cellecia or Emmettin not said anything? Before she could think any further about it, the priest once again moved to the fire. He began to circle the flames in a clockwise direction and this time his chanting was louder, though no clearer. After the three circles, he threw the powder into the flames but instead of the green, the flames flared higher than they had previously and turned white. At that moment, the sun crested the high mountain peaks and the world was bathed in light. He once again took up the brand and pulled it from the fire, this time the round disk on the end was a shining white. He came toward her and Lahnni sat still. She would not fight the process, she just wanted it done.

She clenched her free hand as the brand came down on her inner wrist. The hiss of the skin and the smell of burning flesh filled the air around her. She screamed again as the brand felt like it lanced through to her core. Lahnni screamed over and over as the priest chanted and pressed the brand harder onto her. She felt something rise within her and a flash of blinding light like a door had been opened, but it disappeared just as quickly as if someone had slammed the door on the inviting light. With those final images, Lahnni's head fell forward, the only reason she didn't fall from the chair was the hands holding her in place at her shoulders.

The brand was removed and the crowd grew silent as they waited for the priest to declare her symbol. Kahlahnni looked at her arm and was bewildered by what she saw. She quickly looked to the priest who she found staring at it, his lips pursed with concentration. The kind-voiced soldier who appeared to be in charge came to stand next to the priest and Lahnni watched his face grow still as he took in her symbol. She caught the look the soldier and the priest gave to each other before the priest turned to the crowd. "As some of you have suspected she is a Roamer." He looked at her wrist again and frowned. "Sometimes their brand is stubborn, much like its caste. I should have anticipated that from her appearance alone," he said to the soldier, who nodded.

And with those words, he waved his hand and the soldiers let her go. Someone handed her a wet cloth but did not help her drape it over the wound as they had the others. Lahnni stood and took in the faces of the crowd, if anything they were more hostile and she had no understanding of why that would be. What she did know was that she was a Roamer and there was no one else in the town that was a part of that caste. Then understanding dawned on her. She did belong somewhere. Just not here.

Chapter 5

The emotions engulfed her from every side and Kahlahnni felt as if she were drowning in them. The branding had clearly increased the townspeople's feelings, with the anticipation of the event moving into the hysteria they had all witnessed when Traiss, the inn keeper's daughter, had not been made instantly into the secret royal she thought she was and onto the spectacle that had been the revelation that Lahnni was a Roamer, though she still didn't understand what that was and why she was feeling that it wasn't acceptable at all. From what she was feeling, they would have been more comfortable with her being revealed as a servant, stuck in servitude for the rest of her life. It was discomforting to know that Roamers were not wanted and Lahnni wondered why she had never seen one.

Emmettin and Cellecia approached her, their faces mirrored each other, both filled with concern, but also relief. "Are you okay?" Cellecia asked as they got closer.

Lahnni nodded, not trusting herself to speak. She was confused on many levels and didn't know what she wanted to ask first.

"Can I see the brand?" Emmettin asked.

Carefully Lahnni peeled off the now slightly pink cloth. The blood from the harsh branding had seeped into it. Both of her guardians studied her arm before they exchanged a silent glance.

"Is there something wrong?" Kahlahnni asked as she placed the damp cloth back over it.

"It looks like the Brand of the Roamers," Emmettin answered. "But it is slightly off."

"Great," muttered Lahnni. "I can't even get branded correctly."

"Let's see what it looks like when it heals. The Priest did press down unnecessarily hard in my opinion," Cellecia said, as always the voice of reason. "I think half the time they like to build the drama which is why he left you and Traiss till last. We all knew the girl had delusions of being more than what she was and then you were going to cause an issue regardless of what you were revealed as. All the extra powder and changing the smoke color to white to show how hard he had to work to channel the Gods will was all for making him looking grander."

"What are Roamers?" blurted Lahnni; she had a growing need to know.

"They are a race of people who travel the river system and roads of Segarris," Emmettin explained without the rancor she felt from the townspeople. "They tend to stay within their family groupings, and while welcoming of strangers, they keep their secrets hidden. Many of them are entertainers, and they travel in their groups setting up big tents outside of the towns for the people to visit and watch acrobats, sleight of hand acts, and other entertainments."

Lahnni pondered all this as the soldiers started walking amongst the still gathered crowd asking them to move on so things could be packed up and they could make preparations to move onto the next town for the priest to perform the branding rituals there. By the time the soldiers and the priest got to the end of their assigned cities, towns, and villages, it was probably time to start the circuit again as the next group of young people were ready to be branded.

The three of them began to walk down the main road of the town toward the bakery. Lahnni knew there was more to the Roamers than what she was being told, by the senses she was picking up from the crowd, but how was she going to communicate that without raising suspicion? "Why have they never come here?"

Emmettin looked around as if making sure no one was listening to him. "We are too far away from any major river system or main highway to warrant their attention. The town is relatively small and with the farms so spread out there is not enough coin for them to bother to come here."

Cellecia also looked around before she chimed in. "Sometimes I think the townspeople speak so poorly of the Roamers because they feel snubbed that no one bothers to come here."

"They are xenophobic fools who can't see beyond their small lives," Emmettin's voice filled with disgust.

Any further talk was interrupted by Margueritte running up the road to greet them, she carried her youngest sibling while dragging the middle one along behind her. "What happened?" she demanded.

Lahnni looked to the two adults for guidance. She still wasn't sure why she hadn't been told what she was before now, but they obviously had a reason and they had been good to her and she wasn't about to say anything she shouldn't in front of Margueritte. She decided the best thing to do was let them explain what they wanted to.

"It was all very exciting. Traiss carried on when she wasn't revealed to be a long-lost princess," Lahnni diverted Margueritte by changing the subject slightly.

The younger girl grinned wickedly. "I wish I had been there."

Kahlahnni was tired and confused, and with it being Rest day she didn't have work until later when she was expected to help clean out the bakery with the family as they did every Rest day afternoon. She didn't want to go home and face questions and pretend that she was okay. She needed solitude where she could think about everything that had just happened.

"Would it be okay if I take a walk to clear my head?" she asked Cellecia.

"You don't need to ask permission. You are an adult now." Cellecia's voice was sad.

Lahnni didn't understand why, but she nodded her understanding. "I will be back by lunch."

Margueritte handed her sisters to her parents and hurried over to Lahnni who had walked away. "Lahnni, you going to the mill?" she whispered.

"Yes. I just need to think, but when I get back we can talk about what happened. Okay?"

The younger girl smiled brightly. "Okay." She skipped away happily.

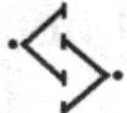

Being Rest day, Lahnni was confident that she was not going to be discovered in the local mill's barn. The miller kept tools and his horses in the lower section of the barn while the second floor, which was about half the size of the lower level, held sacks of what she assumed was grain. There were no horses currently in the barn, Lahnni had passed them lazing under a large tree in the paddock adjacent to the mill. She settled into her favorite hiding spot and removed the now dry cloth from her arm. A few places had dried blood and now she had made it sluggishly bleed again as she tugged at the cloth. Folding the stiff cloth as best she could, she placed it on the thin layer of hay that covered the floor and then put the shuttered lantern she had taken from the table on the lower floor next to it. Carefully, so nothing would catch fire in such a flammable environment, Lahnni opened the lantern and cautiously lit the wick with the flint she always carried in her pocket. It had become second nature to carry a flint to start a fire as most mornings she arrived at work well before Marggot and needed to get the fire going. On one occasion Lahnni couldn't find the flint to light the fire with and had received a whipping for not having it lit when Marggot arrived, after that she carried her own to avoid another whipping. She always suspected that Marggot had deliberately hidden the flint to get her in trouble.

With the lantern now casting a little more light and after hesitating for a few more seconds she swallowed hard, told herself to get it together, and looked at the symbol that now marked her arm and that she would carry forever.

It was nothing like the other marks she had seen. Two V shapes were lying on their sides, opposite each other. Their pointed sections faced outwards and had a dot near the point. The right hand V was slightly higher than the left hand one and each end of the V had a short straight line. She stared at it for a long time and wondered what it was supposed to look like if the Priest had got it right. Every other brand she had seen always had a long straight line somewhere, but not this.

"So, this is the symbol of a Roamer," she said to no one. "And I am a Roamer."

Lahnni had mixed feelings. It was a relief to know that she was not alone, that there were people just like her out there, but did she want to leave the only place she knew, no matter how hostile, to find who knows what outside of her town? The thought was more than a little daunting.

As she lay in the hay with her thoughts and a jumble of emotions that she was struggling to sort through, she had a moment that made her sit up quickly and then scramble to her feet as she felt an urgency overcome her to know the answer. If she was a Roamer, where was her family and how had she ended up here, and was there anyone in town keeping that secret? Could someone at the Boarding House tell her anything? How old had she been when she was brought in there? Did Cellecia know more than she was willing to admit?

In her haste to find answers to the constant stream of new questions appearing in her mind, Kahlahnni had forgotten the cloth and the lantern until she was halfway across the mezzanine that stored all the miller's grain.

Letting out a huff of annoyance at herself, Lahnni turned and headed back to her spot. As she bent to grab the forgotten lantern she heard a scraping of sound, like a boot on the floor, followed by a polite cough. She straightened slowly, picking up the lantern, and turned, what she found made her heart lurch.

"Hello, Creeper." Ambrosse's voice was bemused, his pale gray eyes sparkled with unconcealed delight in finding her alone.

Lahnni felt ill. This was bad. This was very bad. She was trapped. Ambrosse stood in front of the ladder that led down to the lower floor. She had been so clearly caught in her own emotions she had not felt him approach.

"Just like old times." He smirked at her.

"What do you want?" She tried to keep the fear from her voice.

He laughed mockingly. "You know I did my training near the Twin cities and I have met your kind." He looked at her up and down in a way that filled her with dread. "You are just like the rest of them; arrogant. Walking around like you are better. Like your God is grander than everyone else's." He took a step closer to her. "Just like when we were younger, you still need to be taught a lesson."

"Ambrosse, what do you want?"

"I want you to know that just because you have been branded you haven't escaped me."

Lahnni watched him but also was desperately trying to find a way to get around him. She was feeling more and more trapped as she realized that the grain sacks would hinder any attempt of making a run for it. "How did you find me?" she asked, hoping to distract him and give herself more time to figure out what to do.

"The young girl, Margueritte, was happy to tell me where you were. Which was a little disappointing. Bullying her a little would have been fun, but no, she was thrilled to accommodate a soldier who just wanted to check on you. I guess having her dad in uniform makes her too trusting in some aspects."

The way Ambrosse said Margueritte's name made Lahnni feel ill. There was something wrong with this man. There always had been. She flexed her hand and felt the stiffness of her thumb and remembered the sheer glee he had shown as he broke it the final time she had defied him as a child. He took another step toward her and she struggled to maintain her composure and not try to dash around him. It was too risky, there was every chance he would lose control and just push her off the side of the second story floor. He was too unpredictable. Lahnni had to figure out another way to get around him.

"Why don't you just tell me what you want?"

Ambrosse laughed loudly. "Where would be the fun of that?" And with those words, he closed the gap even more between them. "I can do whatever I like to you and no one will believe you, they will believe me. I could cut your hair again or break all the bones in your hand, and if I said it was an accident or that you wanted me to, no one would call me a liar. No matter what I did, they wouldn't believe you." He looked at her neck and licked his lips, making her understand just how deranged he was. She remembered that moment so long ago where he had licked the drops of blood off her neck from the cut he had caused as he sheared off her hair. She still had that small scar under her ear. It took all of her control to not reach up and hide the scar or shudder at the thought of his tongue against her. His next words brought her back to the danger she was in. "I could strangle you until you passed out, have my way with you, and then tell everyone you were begging for it and no one would disagree." He barked a short, sharp hollow laugh. "You are a Roamer and in a town like this, you will always be the outcast. There is no fear of repercussions like there are elsewhere so we can take our disgust out and parade it without fear of retribution."

"I would be believed. Emmettin would believe me and he carries more rank than you," she countered, her voice cold.

Ambrosse shrugged his huge shoulders as if her words carried no threat to him. "Then I shall just have to kill you and make it look like an accident. But first, you will pay for every time you defied me." His voice dripped with malicious intent.

Kahlahnni felt something shift within her. It was as if she could see a long path with a fork in the road just up ahead and she was hurtling towards it. By instinct, she knew what was occurring and she was no longer afraid. This was the beginning of the vision she had experienced all those years prior. He would die today if she could not turn him from his path, and if she was brutally honest with herself, Lahnni wasn't certain she should even bother to try. She wondered how many other younger, vulnerable people Ambrosse had threatened, tormented, tortured, or by his idle death threat before, even killed. How had he been recruited to the military? Wasn't the branding ceremony supposed to weed the supplicants out who were not suited to certain castes?

"Touch me and you will die," she warned.

He sneered at her but didn't move any closer. "How are you going to accomplish that?"

"I warned you when you broke my thumb that you will die a horrible death if you remained on your current path. This is the moment, this is your choice. Walk away and you live, attack me and you die," she said with no emotion as if she predicted people dying all the time and it was no big deal.

"You Roamers always be claiming to have abilities like healing, killing silently, or telling the future, but we all know you are charlatans. All you do is take money from good people and tell them what they want to hear or give them healing herbs that are just tea leaves." He scoffed. "You don't frighten me." And with that, he grabbed for her.

Kahlahnni had been ready for it. Emmettin had taught her to stay alert when cornered and to seize the moment when it came because if you were patient enough there would always be a chance to do something in the hope you could get away. It might not always work, but you at least had a shot. As Ambrosse's arms reached for her she ducked low and ran straight for his midsection, tucking her head and angling her shoulder to hit him in the middle of his ribcage. The strike wasn't enough to knock him down, but it did take the wind out of him and he bent forward as he took in a huge gulp of air. Without hesitating, Lahnni swung the lantern she had been holding and hit him in the side of the head. The lantern shattered and he fell to the ground. Lahnni didn't look back as she jumped over him and ran to the ladder. It was only then did she look back to make certain that he was not following her and realized that the broken lantern had caught fire to the hay spread on the floor and was spreading rapidly up the sacks of grain. Blood poured from the gash on Ambrosse's forehead as he turned to look at her. His gray eyes piercing her soul in their hatred of her.

She grasped the ladder and hurried down the rungs, slipping several times in her haste and continuing to look up. Lahnni was two-thirds of the way down the ladder when she looked up to find his foot just starting to move over the landing edge in search of the first rung. She had run out of time. Without conscious thought Lahnni held tight to the sides of the ladder and jumped backward, pulling the ladder with her as she fell. The momentum of the action brought the ladder down on top of her, and she landed funny, twisting her ankle in the process. She looked up from her sprawled position on the floor to find Ambrosse peering over the side, his glare was terrifying in its ferocity.

Thick smoke filled the top of the barn, obscuring the roof, and she could see the red glow of the fire spreading down the walls. Ambrosse coughed and wiped the blood from his eyes as it ran from his heavy gash. "Put the ladder back up, Creeper," he ordered.

Lahnni didn't answer; instead, she pushed the ladder off herself and stood gingerly. She hobbled on her painful ankle, taking several steps backward until she reached the side door she had used to sneak in. Her eyes didn't leave her tormentor's furious face.

Ambrosse stood, his face covered in blood, surrounded by flame, a look of pure hatred aimed towards her. And just like her vision, he was falling, his mouth wide in a silent scream as burning wood splintered around him as the floor gave way. With a thud that could be heard over the now crackling fire, he hit the ground, his neck twisted and he died just the way she had seen.

In complete shock and with no clear thought, Lahnni knew she had to go now. No one would believe her if she said he had tried to attack her and she had only been protecting herself. *That's because you let him die,* her inner voice whispered. *You could have saved him.*

And with those words echoing in her head, she crept out of the burning barn as fast as her ankle would allow and slipped into the surrounding forest with nothing more than the clothes on her back.

Chapter 6

It was unusually hot and her throat was dry. She could still smell the acrid smoke as it was carried over the high treetops of the dense forest by a soft breeze. She silently prayed that the fire was brought under control before it moved into the nearby paddock and hurt any of the workhorses. Lahnni guessed by the angle of the sun and a rough estimate of how long she had been hobbling along that it was after lunch. The rumbling of her stomach seemed to confirm that notion.

The forest was not somewhere she had spent a lot of time since moving to the town after the Captain had "bought" her from Lord Channing of Burrop. Between working in the laundry, helping at the house, and taking care of Margueritte and her sisters so Cellecia and Emmettin could work long hours in the bakery, it left little time for other activities. The teenagers of the area were known to sneak off into the forest to meet up and have gatherings without the overbearing watchful eyes of their parents around. As none of the teenagers had ever been anything other than indifferent or nasty to Lahnni she had never been invited to any of the impromptu parties.

All of these thoughts wafted through her mind as she walked, but nothing truly stuck for her to grasp onto. It was as if her brain had shut down and her emotions had been dulled. Her overpowering desire at the moment was simply to find a large, thick stick that she could use to lean on and take some of the pressure off her ankle and to find the trickling water she could hear in front of her but felt like she would never reach.

Her ankle ached and her wrist throbbed. She was miserable, confused, and scared, but there was no guilt and she had no idea how to feel about that. So many things had happened in such a short amount of time that Lahnni needed to think about, but at the moment easing her dry throat and washing her dirty, bloody wrist were her priorities.

She caught the foot of her bad ankle on a small rock and yelped as she fell forward, grazing both knees and ripping her skirt as she landed heavily. Holding back tears, Lahnni struggled to her feet and hobbled over to lean against a tree. Placing her back against the wide trunk to steady herself, she gathered her now dirty skirt and held it to one side so she could look down and inspect her knees. One knee was just grazed, the skin white from cuts but not bleeding, the other knee was far worse, with several cuts across the knee cap that was bleeding slowly. Lahnni picked out a few small stones and brushed off the dirt as best she could, adding her knees to the list of reasons she needed to get to the running water that she could hear.

Straightening up, Lahnni dropped her skirts and went to push off from the tree trunk when she noticed to the right of her there was a thick stick lying on the ground that looked like it could be the perfect height to use as a walking cane. She had got the idea to find one to aid her in walking from the Lady Aisllyn, who had used one to help her walk when her hips and knees were aching and sore. The disease of the ancient, Lady Aisllyn called it. Gingerly, Lahnni stepped to the right and lent over to grab the stick, bending over to grasp it and then used it to help her stand up again. It was perhaps a little long for her shorter height, but it would do.

With the aid of the makeshift walking stick, Lahnni was able to make better time and kept moving away from her town and up into the foothills of the mountain range that sat to the east of the only place she knew to be home. The sound of what she guessed to be a stream became tantalizingly clearer as time wore on and in what she surmised was another quarter turning the trees cleared slightly and there in front of Lahnni flowed a beautiful, slow-running creek.

Afternoon sunlight fell across the clear water as it trickled around several rocks that jutted out the side of the creek. One of the rocks was flat and looked to be large enough for her to sit on and begin the process of cleaning herself. Finding a spot on the ground that was covered in dry leaves and relatively dirt-free, Lahnni sat down and unlaced her right boot, taking it off and placing it next to her stick. She then took a deep breath and began to unlace her other boot. Pain shot up her leg as she pulled on the laces too hard, but eventually, she got them undone. Her eyes full of tears, she bit her bottom lip and grunted as she tugged the boot off her foot to reveal a swollen, darkening mess. Several tears ran down her face and she wiped them away with the back of her hand. Tears were pointless; they had never helped her and they wouldn't now. The outside of her ankle looked like it had an apple attached to it, the lump was so large. She carefully flexed her foot up and down, it didn't seem like anything was broken, but she would need a few days to know that for certain. The best thing she could do for now was get it into the cold water to help with the swelling so that is what she focused on.

Taking advantage of the fact that she was out in the forest and truly alone, Lahnni made the decision to remove her over-apron and then her dress. She found a low-hanging branch and hung her dress on the end, her apron she managed to tear a few strips off the end of it and then hung the apron with the dress. Kahlahnni stood in her short cotton sleeveless tunic and above the knee bloomers and enjoyed the coolness those fewer layers brought. Tucking her three strips of cloth into the waistband of her bloomers and picking up her walking stick, she made her way slowly onto the bank of the stream; being slower than was necessary, as she didn't want to tumble into the water and risk being injured further.

Eventually, Lahnni made it onto the flat rock and settled onto her bottom, and then carefully inched out so her twisted ankle could lay in the running water while she bathed her other wounds. Firstly, she carefully leaned over the side and cupped her uninjured hand and scooped up as much water as she could, bringing it to her mouth again and again until her thirst was gone. Now she could focus on her wounds. Taking one of the strips of cloth, she wet it and wrung it out before she dabbed gently at her bloody knee. It didn't take long to remove the blood around the cuts as it wasn't sore, so more pressure could be used. With greater care, she gently cleaned the cuts and made certain there was no debris left in there to fester. She inspected the other knee to find the whiteness had disappeared and her typical more olive tones had returned.

Kahlahnni dipped the next strip into the cool water and enjoyed the feeling. There was something cleansing about the feel of the water running through her fingers. She had never been into anything larger or deeper than a half-filled bath barrel and had stayed clear of the larger sections of river that ran along the side of the town as it looped around after originating from the higher mountains. This smaller stream could be an offshoot of it and possibly was the same one that ran at the back of Lady Aisllyn's estate manor.

She held her hand, wrist up, out over the water and put the soaking cloth on the branded area, hissing at the sting it caused. Lahnni absently watched the water that dripped from the cloth, even with the birds, other critter noises, and trickling water something was missing and she couldn't shake the feeling now that she had stopped moving.

As she sat and took a breath in and slowly allowed it out again, Lahnni registered what had been niggling in the back of her mind for the past few turnings. There was no one else's emotions intruding on her, no one else's fears, anxieties, hopes, or dreams, just her own jumbled feelings. She closed her eyes to enjoy the sensation when she was assaulted by the vision of Ambrosse's face covered in blood and leering at her. She snapped her eyes open and drew in a ragged breath. She shoved down all the thoughts that came with that vision and tried to focus on deciding what she would do next.

Lahnni looked out across the narrow shallow stream to the forest beyond and saw the beginnings of the steeper side to the mountain range. *There has to be some sort of cave in there that I could sleep in tonight while I figure out what I want to do,* she thought to herself. She decided it was probably best to find a cave now rather than keep walking and hope to discover one later and not have enough time to find firewood. She needed to be practical and keep her fear under control by focusing on the now. And at the moment the most important thing she needed was shelter and to rest her ankle.

Almost unwillingly, Lahnni removed the make-shift cloth from the brand and gently patted the flakes of blood that still stuck to the area. Eventually, it was clean and what was exposed was angry, red, raised, and raw. Her eyes traced the double-on-their-side V's with their dots near the outside pointed ends. She stared at it, hoping that in some way she would feel a connection but there was nothing but bewilderment with what it represented. "Where are your visions now?" she said out loud, her voice filled with scorn. She knew that there was no understanding why she was the way she was and she never seemed to have visions just of herself, it always involved someone else, but it still didn't stop her from wishing it were different.

Kahlahnni took out the third cloth strip from her waistband and wrapped it tightly around her wrist tying it in place and tucking in the ends as best she could one-handed. She inched back a little and pulled her foot out of the water and sat there for a few moments longer, waiting for it to dry in the late sun.

Once it was dry, she carefully made her way back to her clothing where she tied her bootlaces together and slung the boots over her shoulder before then placing her dress and over-apron across her shoulders, like a long fur stole, and picked up her stick. With trepidation, she faced the stream and tried to pick a path through the shallowest, slowest moving sections to get to the other side without hurting her ankle more or falling in and becoming drenched.

After a few moments, she decided on her best path and stepped into the cool water. In a shorter time than she expected, Lahnni was on the other side with minimal fuss and still mostly dry. Her ankle throbbed as there had been several moments where her foot had slipped and she had ended up sliding off a rounded rock causing her ankle to twist.

Repeating what she had done on the other side, Lahnni found a relatively dirt-free spot covered in dry leaves and after hanging her skirt and apron from a nearby tree she sat and put her boot back on her good foot. The injured ankle took a few attempts and a lot of swearing but Lahnni eventually managed to get her other boot back on and over her injured ankle, though there was no chance that she could tie it back up, so she tucked the laces into the side of the boot as to not trip over them. She considered not putting her dress and apron back on as she was enjoying the freedom of movement and not being hot in the extra layers of skirt, but realized that she would be better off without them hanging around her neck as she decided to start to carry sticks and twigs to start her fire when she found a suitable spot. Quickly Lahnni completed getting dressed, sighing heavily at the injustice of having to always wear a long skirt, and headed in the direction of the steeper slope of the mountainside.

Kahlahnni continued to stay within sight of the creek, knowing that she would need water to survive and it would be easier if she didn't have to trek far to get it until her ankle stopped hurting. She also decided that if she wanted to, she could possibly turn around and follow it downstream and more than likely it would bring her out at Lord Channing's estate house where she might be able to hide for a several nights and steal a few eggs and other oddments to keep herself going until she figured out what to do with herself. It was only now that she was coming to understand how ignorant she was of the world and of how to truly take care of herself. The unknown was so vast that it was almost paralyzing. Living in such an isolated town for so long Lahnni could almost begin to understand why the townspeople feared change and how her being so different was something to be seen as suspicious. Some had obviously heard talk of Roamers, but what that meant she guessed was all based on super-stition and not their own experiences as they had little or none. Emmettin was probably the only truly traveled man of the whole town and now she wondered why he had chosen to settle there when he had retired from the navy. There were so many unanswered questions.

By the time Lahnni had gathered a small bundle of twigs and sticks that she carried in one arm, while she continued to use the walking stick, and as her ankle grew more painful, she was considering just using an overhanging rock as shelter so she could stop walking. The pain was becoming unbearable. Kahlahnni spotted a darker section on the side of the steeper section of the foot of the mountain and prayed to whatever Gods the Roamers prayed to that it was the opening to a small cave.

As she came closer to the dark patch, she was happy to discover that it was indeed an opening to something. Lahnni moved closer and only halted when she recalled that wild animals lived in the forest and it may be best to be a tad cautious and not go barging into a den of some kind. By instinct, she closed her eyes and ignored the pain of her injured body, instead she focused on listening to her surroundings and trying to sense if there was anything near her. Kahlahnni didn't know if it would work for animals but it was worth a try. She got no reaction from her search, so guessed there was nothing nearby or that whatever her abilities were they didn't extend to animals.

There was only one way to find out for sure, so she placed her small pile of sticks on the ground and moved to the opening; she blinked several times as her eyes adjusted to the dimness and Lahnni could only make out the first few feet of the area. Kahlahnni stopped and waited, figuring that if she had disturbed something it would attack or try to slink out sooner rather than later. While she waited, she balanced on her good ankle and held her walking stick in two hands like a weapon. When nothing rushed for her and she could hear no movement, she decided it would be safe enough to make a small fire right in the entrance to begin with, to provide light, and then she could build a bigger one once she can see further into the space. That way Lahnni wouldn't accidentally trip and hurt herself more—she had had quite enough of that for one day.

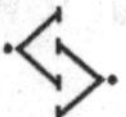

Dark thoughts crowded Lahnni's mind. She was having trouble sleeping, the cave had been wonderful and cool during the day but now that the night had come the air was cooler in the mountain range and the cave was now cold and the ground hard. She wished she had thought about collecting dried leaves to make a bed but it had not been something she contemplated until now. Her only thought had been building a fire that was large enough to warm her, and then to rest her ankle. She had fallen asleep by the fire she had made only to be woken by dreams of Ambrosse burning in front of her and faces laughing as images of her being dragged down the main street in town by her hair filled her mind. She was dragged to the town center where the branding had taken place and left in the middle of a group of jeering people. One by one they stopped their yelling and their faces grew stoney before they turned their back to her. The last in the circle were Cellecia and Emmettin, and Lahnni cried out when they both also turned their back on her, shunning her like the rest. This had jolted her awake and in the cold barren cave, Lahnni began to cry.

Maybe it would have been best if she had just died in the fire with Ambrosse. It was probably what she deserved after not trying to save him.

Everyone is just going to be happy that I am gone, she thought as she lay there sobbing. The ugly one, with her dark features and refusal to be less. She sniffed loudly, trying to get her crying under control. Lahnni didn't like to cry. It meant to her that they had won and she was prideful and stubborn even though she shouldn't be, and refused to allow them the idea of knowing their cruel taunts and harsh attitude bothered her. But now, hidden away and knowing she was responsible for the death of a man, the walls came down and she cried. She cried until she felt sick and drained.

Lahnni cried for the loss of Cellecia and Emmettin. At least they could stop defending their choice to take in the orphan, and Margueritte and her sisters were now safe from persecution by association. They were better off without her and she was better off without them. It hurt to know they had not been honest with her and now she was second-guessing everything they had told her. Had they been trying to keep her ignorant for a reason or because they were also prejudiced and hoping to have her be branded as something other than a Roamer?

Eventually, the tears stopped and numbness again set in. The ache of her ankle and the throbbing of her wrist were reminders of how much bad she had caused, and that she deserved the pain as she wasn't worthy of love. Her eyes grew heavy and she longed for peaceful sleep where she could escape.

At some point, she must have drifted off because the next time she opened her eyes she was looking at the dying embers of her fire. Kahlahnni needed to find more firewood in a hurry or risk having to go through the painstaking task of building her fire all over again. The need to go to the bathroom was also becoming more insistent and she would prefer to do that outside and not in the small space that she was living in. She rolled over to find sunlight peeking through the opening of the cave.

It was difficult to think clearly, Lahnni seemed to be overly hot, especially after the freezing temperatures during the night, and her head pounded. Her branded wrist was incredibly itchy and she needed to go outside to see it in a clearer light and to clean it again in the creek.

Leaning heavily on the walking stick and grunting with the effort Lahnni stood and hobbled out of the cave entrance and into the weak morning sunlight. Birds chirping greeted her and a slow breeze rustled the higher-up branches of the trees above her head. All of this would have made Lahnni smile and stop and enjoy the moment, but her stomach growling ruined the mood and reminded her that she was hungry and it was the first time she really considered how she was going to survive out in the forest. She had clean water and shelter, but food would become an issue soon. But her most pressing issue was relieving herself, so she found a shrub up close to the rock formations, which appeared to be part of the cave, and went behind that. She could not decide why she wanted the cover of the bush when there was no one out in the forest but she guessed it was second nature to be modest when going to the bathroom, regardless of circumstances.

Slowly, Lahnni moved out into brighter sunlight, rather than the dappled sunlight that was coming through the canopy of forest trees to check on her wrist. Red lines are coming out from under the bandage and while it was dirty from lying on the ground there was also what was some sort of discharge coming from the wound that had seeped through and stained the cloth. She had a bad feeling that it was infected, which would explain the fever and raging headache. Lahnni knew that she needed to get to the water and clean as much of the infection out as she could.

Holding her walking stick a little firmer, Lahnni tried to walk quicker. Worry for her wrist overtook her common sense and her foggy brain did not protest as she put too much pressure on her severely swollen ankle—but her body did. Only having taken a few steps, Lahnni's ankle gave out and she stumbled, then tried to hop to right herself but ended up putting her injured foot down, tripping over an exposed tree root, and falling face-first into an unforgiving tree trunk and knocking herself out.

Chapter 7

The smell of cooked fish filled her senses and Kahlahnni struggled to remember what had happened. She lay there for a few moments keeping her eyes closed and trying to sort out what was going on. Something soft was under her head and something was covering her. The warmth of a fire warmed the side of her face and she lay on her back, which was not her normal sleeping position. Her head now throbbed as much as her ankle and she was hot but she shivered as if chilled. There was suddenly a scraping sound nearby and then pressure on her branded wrist. Rapidly, her mind came awake and she opened her eyes in fright.

It was the soldier with the kind voice and beautiful eyes. Lahnni blushed when she realized how close he was to her. Why had she not felt him when she woke up? Was her usual abilities gone or just stunted from her fever? Lahnni should have felt relieved that she couldn't feel someone else but only now came to realize how much it was part of her and how much she had grown to depend on the innate ability to be warned about something even if she couldn't tell what it was. It had only been in extreme situations that the visions had been clear, like the recurring one with Ambrosse or the interview with Lord

Channing before Emmettin had shown up and rescued her. She realized that the only thing she felt from him was competence. He had complete confidence in his abilities to deal with any situation. Emmettin had always felt the same way when she was in his presence.

The man's head was bent over her arm, and he was concentrating on bandaging her wound with something clean but a different color to what her apron was. The soft leather gloves he wore were marvelously cool on her hot, wounded wrist. "I am glad I found you," he spoke softly, causing her to jump. She had not realized he knew she was awake.

"You are?" The words were said before she could stop herself.

He looked up from his bandaging and his aquamarine eyes caught hers, he frowned. "Of course."

"You would be the only one," she said, again without censoring herself.

"I doubt that."

"You were there, you saw the townspeople react to me. Please, don't treat me like a fool. I may be different to everyone, but I am not a simpleton." She couldn't believe she was speaking like this to a stranger.

"Your family, then. I am certain they will be happy to discover you are safe."

She stared at him for a few moments before answering. "I have no family."

"The people you live with?"

Lahnni was wary. He was helping her, but she didn't have her usual senses to rely on whether he was wanting to help or drag her back to face charges of murder. His intent was not clear and neither was her thinking. "The people I lived with are not your concern." She rushed to sit up, but grew dizzy and put her head back down.

"Let me finish this and then I will help you sit and bring you some fish and water." He returned his attention to her wrist and she noticed in the brighter firelight that the red streaks were still thick and winding their way up her arm.

She nodded and shivered even though she could feel the heat from the fire. Clearly, her fever had not broken and the brand site was badly infected. Lahnni went to pull the blanket that was covering her further up to her neck with her good hand and encountered the feel of heavy brocade and a stiff collar. This was not a blanket that was keeping her warm, but what she guessed to be the same cloak he had worn the morning of the branding.

Kahlahnni lay there and thought about the fire she had caused and the death of Ambrosse, one of this soldier's men. Why had he not brought it up? She was confused and her brain seemed to stop being logical but she fought against the fog and tried to remain calm. She certainly didn't want to incriminate herself, but she also didn't know if she could live with the guilt she felt. She watched him expertly tie the ends of the new cloth and realized that the material was the same color as his uniform shirt. "Thank you," she murmured as he stood and moved to the fire where he threw her dirty, contaminated bandage into the flames.

"You are welcome. Would you like some food?"

"Yes, please." This time, with more care, Lahnni raised herself onto her elbows and once her light-headedness passed, she pushed herself up to a seated position.

"Do you need help? I could move you to prop against the wall?" he offered.

"No, thank you. Here is fine."

"How do you feel?" he asked as he carried what she presumed was the aforementioned fish to her on a large round leaf.

"Awful. I am not sure what hurts the most. Everything seems to be mixed in together."

"Between your head and your hand?" he questioned.

"My head?" She lifted her hand and touched the side of her head where the pain seemed to be concentrated, she felt a large lump that was tender to touch. That must have been what she knocked when she hit the tree root. Lahnni took the leaf and smiled shyly with thanks. "My head is probably not helping my thinking, but I am sure it is mostly the fever and infection making my thoughts hazy." As she chewed on the perfectly cooked fish, she rested the leaf in the hand of her injured arm and with her good hand lifted the skirt to reveal her bulging ankle through her boot and her skinned knees, which had been hit again when she knocked herself out by the look of the bloody scabs that had now formed.

His ocean blue eyes, or at least what she always thought the ocean would look like, widened at her added injuries. "How on Segarris did this happen to you?"

She shrugged, not wanting to explain the ankle. "Just extra clumsy."

He gave her a look that she didn't understand and spoke softly. "I have watched you, Kahlahnni, and there is nothing clumsy about you.

"You know my name."

"I know all the names of the supplicants."

"What is your name?"

He sat across the fire from her and began to eat his portion of fish. "I am Sergeant Evannderth, but you may call me Evan."

They sat in silence for several moments, eating their fish. Lahnni finished and put the leaf aside. "Thank you for the fish, Evan." She kept her eyes down out of habit more than anything else. "And for saving me."

"You are welcome, Kahlahnni. I think we need to get you down to the water before it gets dark so we can clean those knees and you can have a drink."

She nodded her agreement and looked around for her stick to help her stand. It was nowhere to be found and then she recalled it was probably still lying where she had fallen earlier that day. "How did I get here?"

"I carried you," Evannderth answered as if it was the most obvious thing, and in hindsight it probably was.

"I was using a large stick as a cane; I won't be able to walk without it," Lahnni explained.

"You can lean on me until we find your stick."

The idea of feeling this man against her made Lahnni feel vulnerable in a different way, a way she couldn't quite articulate. "Okay."

With great care, Evannderth placed his hands under her armpits from behind and pulled her up to her feet. Standing this close made their height difference substantial. By her estimate, he was probably a foot taller than her. He looked down at her and smiled that reassuring smile he had used that day at the meeting where he had made her feel seen. "I think it would be easier and quicker if you let me carry you to the place you fell."

Lahnni considered it and in the end, could not come up with a good enough reason for him to not help her. "If you think it best," she answered.

He scooped her up as if she weighed nothing and cradled her against his chest gently. "Am I hurting anything?" he asked.

"Nothing that can't be endured."

As he moved toward the exit of the cave she got a sense of someone else. She could feel annoyance and sourness coming from close by. "Stop," she whispered.

He obeyed instantly.

"There is someone out there." Lahnni felt flustered. "I don't want to see anyone." Her voice sounded as frightened as she felt.

Instead of convincing her otherwise or asking awkward questions, Evannderth put her gently on her feet, close enough to the wall so that she could use it for support. "I am going to need my cloak."

He quickly tucked in his torn shirt and then placed the cloak over his shoulders and buttoned up the tight-fitting collar. Evannderth placed his fingertip to his lips as a signal to remain quiet. Lahnni nodded her agreement; she had no intention of revealing that she was in the cave. Evan moved out of the cave.

"Sir, did you find her?" She heard what could only be described as a younger man's voice ask with enthusiasm.

"Private, what are you doing out here?"

"Brother Sittiq sent me to find you. He wants to move on."

"Has he ascertained how Private Ambrosse died?" questioned Evannderth.

"The town doctor and priest both believe he slipped and fell and started the fire in the process. One of the girls that live with the Roamer says she told Ambrosse that the Roamer might have been in the barn. Maybe he went looking for her?"

Lahnni bit her lip. She hoped that that is what people believed.

"I am certain that Ambrosse probably did just that. I know that he bothered the Roamer at the supplicant's meeting."

"The townspeople want her punished. They think she had something to do with the barn burning. There are mutterings of distrustful Roamers and that she has always found ways to be defiant. Brother Sittiq questioned the family who housed her, and aside from the girl talking about Ambrosse they are very tight-lipped about the situation and how they came to own a Roamer." The words fell out of the Private's mouth. He was talking quickly as if trying to impress his leader with everything he knew.

Kahlahnni could feel nothing but a need to impress from the Private. Evannderth felt confident and in control. Both sets of emotions were weaker than what she typically felt, especially as at her heightened emotional state she would normally get a deeper reading. This made her worry that she could be missing something vital. She also could not see what was happening beyond the cave, only hear the voices. Evannderth could be signaling something different from what his words were saying. With her foggy head, high temperature, and aching body it was difficult to think clearly.

"Okay, we know what sort of person Ambrosse was and he is no loss to the corp or Segarris. Probably why

Brother Sittiq doesn't care to uncover more, regardless of what the townspeople want," Evannderth sounded calm and decisive. "I want you to return to the town and tell the priest to prepare to leave. I will be along shortly."

"And the girl? What do I say?"

"Tell anyone that asks that I found where she slept in a cave last night, but that was after I found her body, or what was left of her at the bottom of a ravine, not far from here. It was hard to tell as I am pretty sure coyotes got to it. She more than likely slipped and fell." Evannderth's voice was emotionless as if he was talking about nothing of interest.

Lahnni's blood ran cold as the implications of his word set in. He had just told the private that she was dead and where to look for her body. Did he plan on killing her himself and tossing her into that ravine? Panic filled her, but she was caught. She had no intention of revealing herself to the private and she wasn't in any condition to escape two of them. She had a better chance of fleeing one. Gritting her teeth and ignoring the pain that coursed up her leg, Lahnni limped to where Evannderth had prepared the fish and was relieved to find what she had been hoping for. His knife.

It was a slow agonizing wait for him to return. By the time Evannderth entered the cave she was sweating profusely and her body was shaking with the effort to remain upright. Lahnni was lightheaded and her thirst unbearable. Her thoughts were jumbled, she couldn't sense danger but had heard his words.

Evannderth walked into the cave, carrying her walking stick, and he halted when he saw her. "He is gone, you are safe." The kind voice he used to talk to her was again present. She wouldn't be fooled.

Lahnni cleared her sore throat. "Give me the stick."

A frown appeared on the blond man's face but he didn't argue, he took a few steps closer and held out the stick. Lahnni took it and leaned it on the dirt floor, feeling an instant relief as she lifted her injured ankle off the ground a fraction to relieve the pressure. "Kahlahnni," Evannderth said softly.

"No," she cut him off. She struggled to keep her hand, which held the knife, from shaking. "I didn't let Ambrosse kill me and I won't let you either."

"Ambrosse tried to kill you?" His voice was not as surprised as it should have been—or was she not hearing properly? It felt like there was a drum pounding in her head. He took a step toward her.

"No," she repeated with more conviction. Lahnni weakly brandished the knife. "I thought you were different, but you're just like Cellecia and Emmettin, you appear to be one thing but, then say something else."

Lahnni blinked rapidly trying to clear her vision. Was the fire growing dimmer? What was she trying to say? Why was Evan looking at her oddly? It was all too much, she just wanted to sleep. And with her mind growing more confused, the knife slipped from her fingers and her knees bent without her permission and her eyes would no longer open.

Chapter 8

Delicious cold water dribbled into her mouth and Lahnni coughed, waking herself up. She went to move but something on her shoulder kept her from sitting upright. Kahlahnni struggled weakly against it. "Would you stop fighting, please?" the kind male voice asked.

She felt a sense of urgency and couldn't explain why until a moment later her jumbled memories came back. "Not Ambrosse, not Lord Channing, and not you." Her voice was rough, but her words clear.

Immediately the pressure on her shoulder was lifted. "Why do you keep saying that?"

"You said I was dead." Lahnni forced her eyes open and glared at him. It was difficult to see properly as the sun was in her eyes and he was behind her and she realized her head was in his lap.

"Do you want to go back to town? I thought you were out here because you were running away from all those small-minded bastards who would have cheered at all the pain you went through at your branding if it wasn't such poor form to cheer at a supplicant's suffering."

"You could have just said you couldn't find me."

"No, that would have caused complications. We need to be moving onto the next town, and I need to know you are safe from some ill-conceived idea of retribution they would create about Ambrosse's death once we were gone. You are a Roamer and they will think you are capable of many things, like the legends of old, which is where their superstitions come from. They will seek you until they know you are dead, if there is a chance you are hiding out here they will continue to hunt for you. The mob mentality will be strong for a while and I can't protect you. So by claiming you dead I thought I was doing what you wished and was also keeping you safe." He looked down at her and she was lost in his eyes for several moments. "I can always go back and say I was mistaken and that you are alive or I can carry you back to your family. I am certain your family will be happy when I tell them you are safe," he insisted for the second time that day.

"I told you I don't have a family." The words came out bitter. "I thought I did, but the more I think about it the more I come to understand that they bought me from my former master, not to rescue me, but to use me for their convenience. I was their live-in childminder when I wasn't working in one of the local laundries that special-ize in fancy clothing. I never worked in their own shop, a bakery, as I can see now that that would have been bad for their business. I was only ever allowed in the back of it to help scrub it clean." That realization hurt more than her injuries combined. She was truly alone in the world. No safe place where she was accepted for herself. That had been a false sense of safety that was now revealed for what it truly was. A farce. She glared at him. "You will not tell them anything, it is best everyone thinks I am dead."

He looked sad but said nothing more. He dipped the white cloth he had been holding into the stream that ran beside them. "Drink," he ordered and brought the sopping material to her lips so she could suck on it, but not take in too much at once.

"You do know I could have killed you when I found you passed out under the tree?" Evan said casually as he looked down at her and raised a pale eyebrow. "If I wanted you dead then you would be dead."

Lahnni opened her mouth to protest before she realized that what he had said was true. "But you said..."

"I have explained why. You either need to choose to trust me or not."

"Then why help me?" Her voice was stronger as the water eased her discomfort.

"Why wouldn't I? You were harmed under my watch and from the pieces I can put together you were attacked by one of my soldiers. That makes you my responsibility, no matter how much Brother Sittiq wants to move on to the next ceremony."

Kahlahnni was silent. She had never been anyone's responsibility.

"What do you want to do? You can't hide up here forever. Someone is bound to find you."

What did she want to do? It was a question she had never asked herself. "I don't want to stay here." The words were out of her mouth and she understood how often she thought about what she didn't want, but never what she did want. Lahnni wondered why.

"Where do you want to go?"

She hesitated for a moment as her understanding of how naive she was became evident. "I don't know. I don't know anything about the world beyond where I have lived." She looked up at him. "Where do you think I should go? You have seen the world. I don't even know what I am." Her voice caught on the last few words.

"You are a Roamer, and they are accepting and kind, though known to be eccentric. The closer you get to the bigger cities of Segarris the more you will find them traveling along the road or on their boats. Many are entertainers and that is the way they make their living."

"Will I find a place amongst them?" She tried not to sound frightened.

"I think you will. You have some skills that you can barter for a place at their fire. The older women are always looking to find more people to mother." He took the cloth and dipped it back into the cool water before handing it back to her. "Once you are a little stronger and we have rid your body of the infection the branding has caused we will head to Pessac, it is the largest town in this region and typically as far north as the Roamers ever journey."

"We?"

Evannderth smiled down at her. "Yes, we."

She wanted to ask why but he shifted under her head and spoke briskly. "Do you think you can sit up? I want you to dangle your ankle in the cold water while I wash your wrist and knees."

"Yes." Lahnni let Evan help her into a sitting position. With effort and a small amount of swearing she managed to tug off her unlaced boot, her swollen ankle now a deep purple as the bruising had begun to appear. She sighed with relief as the constant pressure of the boot eased and she slid her foot into the cool water.

"How do you feel?" Evan asked as he untied the bandage he had put around her wrist earlier.

"Hungry, light-headed, cold, hot." She shrugged. "My brain doesn't seem to want to think clearly."

He didn't touch her arm or the wound he just stared at it for a few moments before he re-tied the cloth. "Let me look at your knees." She shyly raised her skirt to expose her bloody knees. "That is mostly superficial. Do you think you can clean them up while I collect firewood and catch you supper?" He held out the cloth she had been sucking water from.

"I am sure I can manage." Lahnni watched him walk away to begin looking for firewood. She turned her attention to her battered knees and the rivulets of blood that had traveled down her shins. It didn't take her long to clean them up and once she had she could see they weren't bad, and left alone would scab and heal, leaving a very minor scar. But what human didn't have scars on their knees from childhood falls?

She went to wash out the blood on the strips when Evan's voice stopped her. "Don't do that. Leave them out to dry. I have an idea of what to do with those. I am going to need a piece of your dress too, and a boot."

Lahnni turned to look up at him and found him standing close to her with the knife she had brandished at him earlier tied tightly around the end of a slender pole with one of his own boot laces. Her heart jumped for a moment in fright and then she reminded herself of his words. *He could have killed you whenever he liked, why would he do it now?* She took a deep, steadying breath and hoped he had not seen the fear in her eyes.

Doing what she was instructed, Lahnni laid out the strip of cloth from her over-apron with the dull brown blood from her knees still very much evident. Next to it she put the boot that didn't fit her because of her ankle, and then after using her teeth to start a tear at the hem, she tore a ragged piece of material from her ceremonial dress. All three requested items lay in a neat pile for Evannderth to do with what he wished. She had been focused on her task and had not been taking any notice of what he had been doing until she heard splashing. Looking over to the stream, Lahnni was shocked to find the man standing in the center of the slow-running clear water with his trousers rolled to above his knees and his shirt off. He held the makeshift spear up in triumph and grinned proudly at her as he pointed to the fish he had just caught. Evan waded his way to the shore near her and he placed the fish on a few wet leaves he had arranged for this reason. He then moved back into the water in search of another fish.

Kahlahnni sat mesmerized by the way his muscles moved. His skin was fair, far fairer than his face that was always exposed to the sun. He was not heavy and bulky like Ambrosse had been, he was trim and his muscles defined. Something stirred in her. It was an odd but pleasant feeling that she didn't understand. Lahnni looked away before he caught her staring and fought herself to not keep looking back at him. Instead, she decided she was thirsty and it would be perfectly acceptable to face the water and cup her hands to drink, if she just happened to be able to see him in the process then so be it.

By the time she had drunk her fill, but not tired of the view, he had caught another two fish and she had cheered his efforts. He sat down on a rock near her and stretched out his long pale legs. He slowly undid the makeshift spear and then expertly gutted and cleaned the three fish. He talked as he completed the task. "After I have you settled back in the cave I am going to take the clothes"—he indicated with his knife the pile sitting beside her—"and drop them over the side of the ravine. If anyone really wants proof they can go looking for it and find a few remnants."

"Okay."

"Then I am going to head into town and get my troop ready to leave. I will see if I can find you new shoes and a warm cloak. Is there anything else you need?"

Lahnni shook her head; it was beginning to hurt again and her thoughts were jumbled. "I am sure you know better than me what I will need."

He looked worried as he watched her. "Kahlahnni, I am going to run the fish back to the cave then come back and get you. Will you be okay to wait here?"

"Yes, I promise not to pass out and fall in the water."

He smiled at her jest as he stood, pulled his shirt back on, and gathered the cleaned fish. "I appreciate the gesture," he quipped, before hurrying away.

Kahlahnni sat numbly, watching the water trickle by, her mind losing a thought as soon as it entered. She could vaguely feel the pain of her ankle but her arm felt like it was throbbing so hard that a vein might burst. The dizziness started again, but she refused to pass out a third time and be rescued by Evan—it was becoming embarrassing.

She was completely focused on just breathing and not blacking out that she didn't hear him approach until he spoke. "Are you ready?"

"Yes," she whispered.

Evannderth bent down and scooped up Kahlahnni as if she weighed nothing and began to walk briskly to the cave. She rested her head against his chest. She cupped her branded wrist with her other hand and carefully supported her bad ankle with her good one. She truly was a mess.

The fire was roaring and the cave well-lit and warm. He placed Lahnni on a pile of dried leaves, which made a crinkling sound but helped keep the cold of the hard-packed dirt from her aching body. She noted a neatly stacked plethora of different sizes of branches, logs, and twigs. As Lahnni settled onto her leaf mattress and scrunched up the shredded remains of her over-apron to put under her head, Evan wrapped the fish in bright green leaves and with the aid of a stick moved some coals and placed the parcels under it before he covered it with the coals.

Through her tired eyes, she watched him put on the cloak. "I will be back as soon as I can. Don't do anything stupid while I am gone."

"Yes, Evan."

"Is there anything else you need, Kahlahnni?"

"Yes."

"What?"

"Call me Lahnni."

He squatted down in front of her, his hypnotic eyes so close to hers. She thought if she wasn't careful she could find herself lost in them forever. *You don't have your usual sense of others, though he has given you no cause, don't do or say anything foolish. If he knew you killed Ambrosse he would haul you into town and demand justice,* Lahnni reminded herself.

"Lahnni." Her name sounded pretty when he said it. "Are you sure you want it this way?"

"Yes. I don't belong here and they don't want me. I need to find where I fit in."

"Get some sleep," he said as he stood up. "Hang tight until I get back."

She was asleep before he left the cave.

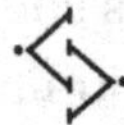

An urgent need to relieve herself was what woke Kahlahnni from her fevered dreams. With special care to not make herself dizzier than necessary, she sat up and waited several moments before she attempted to stand. Her walking stick was still where she had dropped it when she had passed out earlier that day while trying to get away from Evan. Wincing at the throbbing that bending over set off in her head she picked up the makeshift cane and leaned heavily on it, waiting for the intense pulsing to ease.

Lahnni was surprised to find that the sun was only just heading toward the horizon as she emerged from the cave. The forest was duller but there was still plenty of light to see by. She went behind what she had nicknamed the privy bush and took care of what had woken her. She smiled at the silliness of calling a shrub the privy bush, and it felt odd. There was so much to be concerned about and yet here she was making up silly names and smiling to herself.

Her stomach told her clearly what should be her next priority and she did what she was told. Lahnni limped back into the cave and put a few more branches on the fire before using the stick to move the coals and lift out one of the leaf parcels with two smaller sticks like they were tongs she had seen the blacksmith use. She put the parcel down and waited for it to cool before attempting to pick it up. Once it was cool enough to carry she took it outside and settled by the stream to watch the sunset and drink the freshwater while she ate. She didn't dawdle in her eating or drinking as she was aware that her body could decide to stop functioning again at any moment.

As the sun sank below the horizon, Lahnni was back in her cave putting another log on the fire. That small amount of movement had exhausted her and there was no Evan to carry or care for her, so she lay back down, allowing her body to heal and rest.

Lahnni woke turnings later, shivering. She opened her eyes to see that the fire was still burning but needed attention before she went back to sleep or she would wake to find it had gone out. This time she didn't bother to stand; it was too much effort and when she bent over to pick up the wood she knew her head would pound. Holding her damaged ankle off the floor, she scooted on her hands and bottom to the fire. Kahlahnni patiently dug out the second fish parcel and while she ate the still warm white meat she built the fire back up before putting several thick logs on that she hoped would keep the fire burning throughout the cold night. Her teeth chattered and she slowly made her way back to the leaf mattress, wishing her leg was healed as she really wanted a drink, but wouldn't risk hobbling around at night.

Grateful for the heat, but knowing it won't help heal her from the infection that had now moved up to her upper arm, and if it spread much further it would be too close to her heart and too late. As she lay down and her fevered thoughts drifted, she wondered if Evan had left her to die. All the drama that she had created in her head of him attacking her with the knife when in reality he just had to leave her here in this cave and without help, she would die. She had no way of finding her own food and if the fever and infection didn't kill her there were always wild animals and simply starving to death. Lahnni stared at the fire, willing away the macabre thoughts, but they were replaced with Ambrosse's cruel face cutting her hair, licking her bleeding neck, breaking her thumb, all while his voice continually whispered "Creeper."

Lahnni woke over the next day several times, feeding the fire, using the privy bush, and when not fevered and it was light she risked drinking from the steam. But things were becoming dire, the red streaks of infection had now spread across her shoulder and her moments of clear thought were becoming fewer. She was running out of firewood and she was too weak to find more.

Staring at the fading orange coals Lahnni cried softly. She cried for herself, for the pain and isolation she had always felt. For being the strange one, for not belonging, for not having anyone love her the way she saw others love. It hurt to know that she was dying and no one cared. Abandoned by her family and raised by strangers, never fitting in and always being shunned. Maybe it is all she deserved? She never saw visions of herself, only others.

Perhaps because the visions were a curse that had been put upon her for being unworthy? It didn't matter now, she would be dead soon and none of it would matter. The tears ran out and she fell into a stupor.

What sounded like a horse neighing came to her and she knew she was dreaming again. Her mind played constant tricks, she had given up being afraid of sounds that she imagined were coming to attack her. Lahnni didn't even feel curious when she heard footfalls enter the cave. Her senses were completely confused and her visions muddled to the point they no longer made sense.

"Lahnni?" a voice spoke quietly as if concerned it might startle her.

She ignored it, she had heard the voice in her dreams too many times, it wasn't real this time either. Why could they not just leave her alone to die?

"Lahnni?" She remembered who the voice belonged to. A man, a man that said she could trust, but turned out to be like everyone else. He had left her to die.

"Lahnni." The kind voice sounded so concerned. She wished it would go away. She turned her thoughts internally and focused on the pain that coursed through her body. Her wrist was ablaze and searing pain shot up her arm and through her shoulder, her twisted ankle throbbed, as did her head where she had knocked it on the tree. She was drenched with sweat, but her teeth chattered from the cold. She hoped death would come soon, she wondered why she had not been given a vision of it.

Something wet touched her forehead and she flinched. Was it a wolf, come to eat her? Lahnni struggled to open her eyes but failed. She sighed, perhaps it was for the best.

More noises came and she wondered how many wolves there were. *Please let it be quick,* she prayed silently. Nothing happened and her fighting instinct kicked in, the same stubbornness that refused to cower before Ambrosse now forced her to roll over to lay on her back and lift her good hand to rub her eyes. What she encountered was a damp cloth that covered her eyes and forehead, no wonder she couldn't see. Slowly she pulled the cloth from her face and opened her eyes.

There was a shadow of a man near the cold fire, he was feeding tiny twigs into a small flame. Evannderth had come back or was she dreaming or hallucinating? As the flame grew and light-filled the cave, Lahnni took note of the dark coat the man wore and the dark tight-fitting pants that were tucked into knee-high leather boots that looked a little worse for wear. Something caught her eye as he reached out an arm toward the fire, a large band of silver and blue thread wound around the sleeve, where the base meets the cuff. Alarm bells went off in her fuzzy mind, this was not the uniform of Evannderth, she had never seen anything like it. Lahnni realized that she was at the complete mercy of the man, she did not have the strength to do anything but breathe at the moment. The thought was terrifying.

The shadowed man stood and turned to face her and she let out a cry. It was Evannderth, he looked different in his black clothing and he had the beginnings of a blond beard, but she knew it was him, and for the first time since the incident with Ambrosse did she trust her gifts to know she was safe. "You came back." It came out as a croak, but he heard her.

He smiled down at her. "Yes, and I have medicine, food, and a plan."

Chapter 9

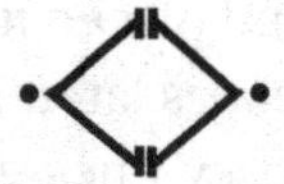

Even after two full sennights the feel of the shiny dark green fabric of her tunic as it slithered over her torso still gave her a slight thrill. Lahnni carefully rolled up the sleeve to expose the now scabbed brand mark, this way the wound could heal quicker without the constant rubbing of the material. She rolled up the other sleeve with less care and more haste as she knew Evannderth would be packing up their camp from the night before by himself and she liked to pull her weight. Kahlahnni tucked the tunic into the waistband of her black full skirt and then sat on a nearby log to pull on the soft black leather mid-calf length boots, grateful that her ankle no longer hurt and the swelling had gone. She put on the tight-fitting black vest and laced up the silver cord that crisscrossed down the front. Giving her head one final shake and dragging her fingers through her damp hair, Lahnni decided she was warm enough without her new cloak and took it from the branch it hung from as well as the small towel she had used to dry herself and a bar of soap. She looked one last time at the slow-moving river; this would be her last bath, Evan had explained, until they reached the city of Pessac approximately ten days from now. He wanted to avoid people so they would stick to the less traveled road.

She picked up the water bottles she had filled and something stuck to the bottom of it, a black feather. She carefully peeled it off and placed it in her skirt pocket to tuck away in her saddlebags later. Lahnni loved feathers, especially the black glossy ones. Feathers gave her the impression of freedom, and the appeal of freedom was intoxicating to someone who had never tasted it. Even now, it was an illusion of freedom she had, what she wanted was complete autonomy and she couldn't do that until she was skilled and competent to live in this world without being beholden to anyone.

Lahnni returned to their campsite to find that Evannderth had packed up both their bedrolls and taken down the cloth they had strung up through branches to give them cover when it rained in the night. It also allowed them to have a fire even when it was wet. The fire was now out and covered with dirt and their horses were loosely tethered to a tree and standing patiently while Evan rechecked their saddles a final time, as he always did before they set out for the day's ride.

Ruby snickered at her as she laid her cloak over the saddle and tucked the soap and towel into one of the saddlebags. As Lahnni ran her hand over the soft tan hide of her beautiful mare, she tensed as she sensed something she hadn't felt since the day after her branding...people. "Evan, there are people nearby," she said softly. Lahnni peered through the heavy foliage of the trees toward the road, attempting to see what she knew to be out there.

"Where are they?" He removed his cloak and laid it over Lahnni's, he then rested his hand on the sword that was belted around his waist.

So Evan couldn't see what she was doing, Kahlahnni turned away from him as if looking for the "noise" of the people she "heard" when in reality she closed her eyes and allowed her power to do what it did without her understanding. She could feel Evannderth, his usual quiet self-confidence still very much present, but there was more. She could sense aggression and boredom from several sources and they were about to enter the clearing by the small trail Lahnni and Evan had used the night before. Kahlahnni didn't think it was wise to speak so raised her hand and pointed to the opening amongst the trees, then held up three fingers to indicate how many people were there.

Three men of varying heights and appearance entered the clearing. If she was less fearful she would have been astounded at how different these men looked to anything she had seen before. Though they look different from each other they all universally had a predatory look on their faces. They were all dressed as uniquely as they appeared and if she didn't feel such a dire warning when she saw them she would have longed to discover more about them.

"You got some ale to spare, stranger?" the closest man asked. He was attempting to sound jovial, but Lahnni could feel the hidden agenda.

"We have no ale or wine," Evan answered. "I suggest you move along." And though he didn't have his uniform on, Lahnni could feel the authority in his voice.

"Don't be like that," the smallest of the three whined. "We just want a little fun."

All three men looked at Lahnni, their intent clear.

"Do you not see my cuffs?" Evan asked.

Kahlahnni looked at the silver thread that wound its way around the top of his cuffs, just like a large bracelet. She didn't realize it had a meaning till now.

The first man shrugged. "So, you are bonded. I don't want to keep her, just have a little play."

"Do you really want the wrath of the Roamers to fall upon you by messing with my bonded?"

"We'll take our chances." Two of the men drew their swords while another brandished a shorter, thicker knife.

Lahnni's heart hammered in her chest. Fear gripped her and she wished she had some way of protecting herself. This was the second time she was in a situation where the ability to defend herself was vital. She had got out of the first one by sheer luck and audacity, this time she doubted she would be so lucky.

"Stay with the horses." Evan spoke quietly as he stepped in front of her and drew his sword.

There was no time for further words as the three men advanced, circling him. Evan was patient, waiting for them to make the first move. Eventually, one lunged and swung his sword, which the soldier easily parried, he then brought his elbow up and drove it into the man's nose, felling the man. Evan continued to move, ducking and parrying as they attempted to engage with him. With a solid kick to the gut of the smaller man holding the knife, he doubled over, giving Evan the moment to bring his sword up and plunge it into the man's chest.

Two down one to go, Lahnni thought, but then she felt something more. Lahnni felt a blaze of anger and it was all the warning she needed. "Evan, behind," she yelled as a fourth man burst through a tall bush, an axe raised in an overhead swing. She watched with awe as in one sweeping move Evan cut through the thigh of the man he had been fighting and continued to turn to face the newcomer, bringing his sword up and in something she had not been expecting, and by the look on the face of the axe wieldier, neither had he. Evan sliced through the wooden handle of the axe, ducking as the axehead went sailing over him and landing in a thicket of brush.

For those brief moments, Lahnni had not been paying attention and hands grabbed her from behind. Arms circled her chest and hauled her off her feet. Panic rose as she was dragged across the clearing, but it was only for a few seconds. He didn't take her far, just out of range of the fighting. She was thrown to the ground and as she landed on her back the wind was knocked out of her, causing her to cough and not be able to scream for help. Lahnni tried to scramble to her feet, but the foul-smelling brute was faster and had her pinned by his much larger arm across her upper chest, with his forearm pushing against the base of her throat, her high collar on the tunic saving her from skin on skin contact. She kicked and scratched, but it had no effect. Her fear was spiraling and she was becoming desperate.

The rancid breath of the filthy man was hot on her face and he grinned at her, his face covered in blood. It was the first man Evan had taken out with an elbow to the nose, he had obviously decided that while her bonded was busy he would take advantage of the situation. He pulled her skirt up with his free hand. His calloused fingers brushed her bare lower leg and a vision forced its way into her mind. She wanted to heave as she witnessed men fighting in what looked like a square box with a rope tied around it. People cheered as the man who had her knocked out his opponent, then the winner ripped off the loose trousers of the vanquished and forced himself into him, rutting like a pig in front of the still jeering crowd. Blood, women, alcohol, and more fighting all flashed into her mind.

Lahnni felt bile rise from her gut as the scenes of this man's violence and debauchery played over and over in her mind. She tried to kick out, raise her head to headbutt him or bite him, but nothing was making a big enough impact to get him to stop. The more she struggled, the harder he pressed against her throat and she fought to breathe, but Kahlahnni wouldn't give up. *You are going to have to kill me before I stop struggling*, she yelled at him in her head.

Abruptly, the man slumped forward and a warmth spread over Lahnni's midsection. The pressure on her throat eased and her screams began to fill the silent glade. As the would-be rapist bled out on top of her, Lahnni screamed, caught in his visions of pain and pleasure. She had never touched anyone as disturbed, not even Lord Channing and Ambrose, who both thrived on others pain. This man was vile.

Suddenly she was free of the visions and the heavy body. Evan had kicked the man off and Lahnni quickly rolled the other way and violently threw up. She wasn't sure if she would ever get those twisted emotions and memories out of her head. Crawling on her hands and knees, she moved away from the man, sobbing.

Someone blocked her path. Evan. He squatted in front of her and held out a cloak. "Take off the vest and tunic." His voice was soothing.

Lahnni did what she was told, but continued to cry. The horror of the brute's breath on her, his heavy body covering hers, knowing that in the end he was stronger and would take what he wanted was terrifying and stayed with her. With numb fingers, she undid the cord of her vest and pulled it overhead, bringing the tunic with it. It was only when she reached for the cloak did she realize that Evan had been a complete gentleman and had held the cloak so no one could see her undress, including himself. Though the only other people around were all dead. She blinked as she took in the knowledge that this kind, considerate man had just killed four people by himself.

A sob escaped her and she huddled in on herself, the images of blood and gore coming back to her. Even though they were now all dead, she felt heavy, surrounded by the hacked-up bodies of the men who were willing to chance the wrath of the Roamer. Whatever that meant. As she cried, Evan picked her up like she was a fragile child and cradled her against his chest, like he had when he had carried her out to the river. This time he quietly talked to her, telling her that it would be okay, that he would protect her, that she was safe.

Evan moved to the horses that were still tied to the tree branch, and took the reins and led the horses, while still carrying Lahnni, down to the place she had bathed in only a short while before. All the while continuing to reassure her.

"Lahnni?" Evan began.

She always liked the way he said her name. "Yes?"

"If I ask you a question do you promise not to panic?"

"How can I promise that?" Her heart thudded. What was he wanting to know?

"True." He paused for a moment. "Can I ask you to trust me? No matter what you tell me, I will believe you."

This made her sit up straighter and stare at him. The firelight danced in his black pupils.

"I will answer your questions if you answer mine," she countered, feeling emboldened by the warmth she saw in his beautiful eyes.

"Three times now you have warned me of people approaching. How do you know that? I am trained for it and I don't hear it until after you do."

Lahnni sat still, watching the flames, not daring to look at him. He was right; she had warned him as the men had approached this morning and again in the midst of the fight when the bandit had attacked from behind. She wanted to tell him the truth; she longed to share her secret with someone. But what happened if he thought her crazy, or worse, he became frightened of her?

"I get feelings now and then about people," she spoke slowly. "If the emotion is powerful enough I get a vague sense of something more."

"Can you remember when your first warning happened?"

"Yes." Her voice was small.

"It's okay, you don't have to tell me." His voice was quiet and full of compassion.

"It was Ambrosse. Any time he was near I would get warnings. He felt bad. Wrong. Not like normal people." She struggled for the right words.

"He had only recently joined my command. I was told to get him in line or send him back for further training." Evan looked at her. "There was something wrong with him. I always felt he took too much pleasure when it was his turn to hold down the supplicant at the branding ceremony."

"I don't know why it happens but I seem to sense if I am in danger." It was a half-truth, but she wasn't ready for him to know that she had visions and that they appeared to come true.

"And you felt in danger around Ambrosse?"

"Always."

"Lahnni, did Ambrosse attack you in the barn?"

Their little camping area was quiet as if even the bugs, birds, and other critters held their breath to see how much she would reveal. "Yes."

"Will you tell me what happened?"

Lahnni closed her eyes and decided that she needed to confess her sin or it would haunt her forever. Evannderth could judge her and decide what her punishment should be. "I killed him."

"I'm sure it was an accident," he reasoned.

"No, I made the decision to not help him and let the barn burn."

"Tell me from the beginning."

Lahnni fought against the visions that wanted to claim her. Her mind wanted her to relive each moment, but she refused to allow it to rule her emotions. "I needed time away from everyone. I didn't understand what had just happened at the branding, but I could feel the fear and spite coming from the townspeople. I always hid in the miller's barn when I wanted to think and be alone, and Margueritte knew it. Ambrosse charmed the information out of her and he came looking for me. He found me up on the mezzanine and told me that he would kill me and that I was to do what he wanted." Her voice was cold and hard as she recounted the events. She refused to let her visions swallow her. "I hit him in the head with my lamp and it shattered, starting a fire on the top level. I managed to get past him and down most of the ladder when he came after me. I jumped from the ladder and brought it with me, leaving him stranded up there with the fire burning. That's how I hurt my ankle. I landed wrong, with the ladder on me. He ordered me to put the ladder back up and I refused." She looked to Evan, and pleaded for understanding with her eyes. "I knew if I let him down he would kill me. He had already told me no one would believe me over him and I knew it to be true. The fire grew too big and the floor gave way. He died when he hit the ground."

"Now I understand why you were so willing to come with me rather than go back to the town."

"Are you going to hand me over to the local lawmen when we get to Pessac?" she asked.

"No. You protected yourself. He attempted to coerce you and threatened to kill you. You were scared no one would believe you, and after what I witnessed with the way the townspeople behaved regarding you I can understand why you believed you would get little support. I am sure if I searched there would be other victims out there. They will all rest easier knowing Ambrosse is no longer with us."

"Really?" She was astounded. Understanding and forgiveness were things she had not expected.

"Yes, really." Evan carefully removed the lid of the one pot they used to do all their cooking and ladled out the hot rabbit stew.

They ate in silence and Lahnni found the quiet peaceful rather than uncomfortable. As she chewed, she thought about how different she felt around Evan as opposed to anyone else. Cellecia and Emmettin had always been kind and she had not lacked for her needs to be met, but there had been a distance and now she wondered if it had been a deliberate decision so she felt like she could not ask questions about herself. It was something to think about later. At the moment she had other questions she needed answered and for some reason, Lahnni felt like this was the right time to ask.

"What did you mean you were bonded with a Roamer, and why would there be a risk in messing with one?" Lahnni took another bite of her stew and waited.

Evannderth watched her closely as if deciding if he should answer. He offered her the rest of the stew. she shook her so he dumped the remainder into his bowl. He ate his food slowly and while Lahnni was tempted to ask another question, she remained patient and waited. Finally, he put his bowl aside and cleared his throat.

"The Roamers, like every other citizen of Segarris, are bound by the country's laws, they also have several laws that are unique to them." He cocked his head to one side and watched her. "One of them is why you were probably safe living in such a xenophobic town. While they ostracised you, they never hurt you because that could incur the swift retribution of the Roamers if it were ever found out. As you learned, there are always people willing to take the risk, but most simple town and village folk talk big but never take the chance."

She nodded at his words, not fully understanding what he said, but coming to realize that her childhood could have been worse if she didn't have that unseen protection. Lahnni recalled the words of Lord Channing when Captain Finnley had come to buy her. He had muttered that it was probably for the best. Perhaps the protection of the Roamers had been the reason he had given up so easily on keeping her in his service.

"And the bond?" she asked.

He held out his arm. "The silver band on my sleeves allows me to wear the clothing style of the Roamers even though I wasn't born one as it tells everyone that I am bonded to a Roamer; in this case, people will assume it is you. Females can also be bonded, but their distinguishing band is around the hem of their skirt if they choose to wear one, or their cuffs, just like a man."

"But what does it mean?"

His aquamarine eyes crinkled as he smiled at her. "It means we are married."

She ducked her head as she felt her face flush. Quietly in the silence of her mind, she had to admit that the thought of being bonded to Evan was appealing.

"It was a better way to travel. Less need for explanation than why a Roamer and a soldier are traveling together. It draws far less attention."

Lahnni raised her head and smiled shyly at him. "It makes sense. Would you tell me more about the Roamers?"

"I am surprised it has taken you this long to ask."

"My life has been difficult and I tried hard to not be noticed and I was discouraged to ask anything, I have come to realize." She didn't keep the bitterness out of her voice.

"I will tell you what I can. Only those who have been accepted into the inner circles of the Roamers understand who they truly are, but I know more than most outsiders."

This caught Lahnni's attention.

"Roamers is the Segarris term for them, they call themselves Pomaikka, it is an ancient word meaning blessed or fortunate. They have always been nomads, rarely settling in one place, always on the move. They trade in goods that can be carried within their wagons. Many are performers and travel in family groups that go from town to town setting up large colorful tents where people come to watch them perform." Evan paused and sipped on his drink. His voice quiet as he went on. "They are also suspected to be assassins and peddlers of truths."

Lahnni gasped audibly; that had not been what she had been expecting to hear.

Evan ignored her shock. "You need to know all of it, not just the good parts. Even though they don't settle in one place, they do have one settlement where all their justice is conducted. It's also supposed to be where they are trained in certain things, if you get my meaning."

"You think that's where they train the assassins and spies?"

"It's a guess, but it would make sense that at least part of their training would be there."

Lahnni nodded. It did make sense. "Is that why people were always suspicious and wary of me?"

"It could be. As I have traveled with the priest for the branding ceremony, I have learned a lot about the different cultures that exist in Segarris and while most co-exist well and have taken on the things they enjoy of others, some have kept to themselves. I find that the further away from a large city, the more close-minded people are to new things, they become stagnant and resistant to change. Which is why it is rare to see anyone but the people from their culture go to those places."

"Doesn't make it right," she said sullenly.

"No, it doesn't." His voice was kind. "But it makes it helpful for you in a way I didn't expect."

Lahnni frowned. "How?"

"The people that hold onto their prejudice also hold onto the past and remember things that the people in the fast-paced city move on from as there is always something new to gossip about. Most of the things they remember are old war tales and slights against them in history, but this time they have also preserved something that may be useful to you."

Lahnni leaned forward, curious as to how the dreadful way she had been treated was relevant to helping her now. *This should be good*, she thought to herself.

"The Pomaikka were once believed to be favored by the Gods and were occasionally born with a gift. Of course, most of the rumors are superstitious nonsense, but now

I am starting to believe there may be some semblance of truth with your admission of ability." He stopped talking and put another log on the fire, poking at it to reveal the hot coal underneath.

"I don't know if you would call me favored by the Gods. My existence has been fairly horrible so far." She said the words in jest, but the truth was there and it stung. If her life was what being favored by the Gods looked like then she would like to be ignored.

"You have had a difficult time and I am sorry for that." He finished with the fire and sat back, resting against his saddle bags. "I was thinking that we might want to change the original plan. Instead of finding a group of Roamers who could take you in and show you their ways, we perhaps seek someone who understands what your brand means and will be able to help you with this ability you have."

Lahnni let out the breath she had been holding. For the first time in her life she wasn't scared of what would happen next. Even though Evan had discussed the original plan with her, while she had been recovering in the cave, it had not felt right, but this did. She looked gratefully at him. "I can't believe you didn't freak out when I told you I could sense things."

He shrugged and grinned at Kahlahnni and her heart beat a little quicker. "I am just glad you were with me this morning to give me that warning when the thug jumped out behind me. Your ability makes you very handy to have around."

Her jovial mood faded as she thought about that morning and the man lying on top of her. Her face must have reflected her mood change. "Don't be afraid. I won't let anything happen to you."

His handsome face was full of something she didn't quite understand, but it didn't matter. What did, was that for the first time in her life she felt like she might be able to trust him to know all her secrets one day.

Chapter 10

The high city walls had been visible for most of the morning and as they rode closer, Kahlahnni's trepidation grew. All the peace she had felt over the last few weeks, learning about the Roamers, building trust with Evannderth, while she regained her strength and her brand healed, began to slip away. The road they were on was linked to a main road that would take them to a large set of city gates. On the road, they were joined by more and more people and the emotions that began to wash over her were becoming more difficult to keep out. She was used to experiencing the occasional emotion by someone in her town if their feelings were heightened and she was close by, but this was almost deafening. She felt people's elation and excitement at reaching Pessac, they were there to make their fortune, see their family or find entertainment in a variety of ways. These emotions she didn't mind, they made her smile and buoyed her mood. It was the dark and hopeless that she struggled with. The people that had come to cause harm, or the ones that had given up on life. Their emotions were oppressive and weighed heavily on her mind as well as physically, making her shoulders sag and her head drop.

She stared at all the people on the road and rejoiced at their breadth of variety. Rich deep burnished skin tones like her own, deepening into the darkest night sky tones that glistened with moisture from the late afternoon heat of the day. Facial features from flat noses, to broad fore-heads, thick necks to thin hooded eyes were all inter-mingled, and if Lahnni had have been told that all these people existed, not just blonde haired, tall, light eyes and skin toned people with their curls, she would have called you a liar. A lifetime she had spent thinking there was no one like her and now she realized there was a whole world not like her and it was okay—because they were all unique and beautiful. She wished she could enjoy the moment and more, but as they drew ever closer to the gates, the cacophony and emotions that poured over the high stone walls felt like they were searching for her.

Kahlahnni's head began to pound and she closed her eyes in the hope it might shield her from some of the onslaught. Not wanting to appear dramatic or silly, she gritted her teeth and struggled on, keeping her head down as if it were a physical force battering at her. Even though it was a warm afternoon, she gathered her cloak around her like it was a shield and huddled under it feeling miserable and longing for the quiet of the forest.

Evan must have called her name several times because he pulled his horse up close to hers and steered them both off the road by having his horse veer in front of hers. "Are you all right?" he asked, his face filled with concern. That warm, kind voice she had come to secretly adore penetrated her foggy mind better than anything else.

It took a few moments for her to find the words. "There are too many people." She looked around to see if anyone was near them or would overhear her words. "There is too much coming in." Her words were strained and he had to bend forward to hear her. "Most people don't bother me, it's only really strong emotions like those men in the woods, but with all these people there are so many forceful emotions. The happy ones are wonderful, but seem to flutter by, the dark, sad ones feel like they are clinging to me and I can't shake them. I am almost struggling to breathe. I can't keep them out." Her whisper sounded more desperate than she had intended and it was only then did she realize how much it was affecting her.

Evan swore under his breath. "That certainly complicates things." He looked critically at her and she grimaced. "Okay, new plan. Do we need to backtrack to give you some relief or can you survive at this distance?"

"I'm not sure. Depends on what you have in mind."

"I am going to leave you here and head into the city. Ask around, check in with the local soldiers and find out if there are a group of Roamers nearby or that have come through recently. I'll get us some supplies and once I know more we can decide what to do next."

Lahnni considered his words and calculated how long it might take him to complete those tasks. She looked around the gently rolling land and spotted a few trees not far to the left. "I could wait under those trees?" she suggested. "I should be okay if I don't get any closer. Are you sure I will be safe?"

"No one would dare to molest you. You are a Roamer, remember. You are out in the open, easily recognizable in attire and appearance. No one is that stupid."

Kahlahnni recalled that Evan had told her that the Roamers were rumored to be assassins and she wondered if that was one of the reasons people left them alone. Though she was scared to be left alone, especially after the attack in the woods, she was more concerned about what would happen to her if she went closer to the large, overcrowded city. She would take her chances waiting under the tree. "Well, the sooner you go, the sooner you will be back." Lahnni gave him a half smile and turned her horse toward the small copse of trees.

It didn't take long to reach the trees and she quickly tethered Ruby to a low-hanging branch before taking off her saddle bags and spreading out a blanket to sit on. From this distance, she couldn't make out individual people, which was a shame as it would have been the perfect opportunity to people watch and see what the citizens of Segarris truly looked like. Lahnni had learned more from Evan in the weeks they had traveled together as opposed to her almost nineteen years in Gennestenmont. Coming to understand that there were three large provinces that had very different cultures and races within, that had once been separate countries but had been united under Arsenny, the First King of Segarris, to stop the bloodshed and warring factions that had threatened to make the continent vulnerable to the vultures of Trioswa. That had been over four hundred years ago, and though there was occasional unrest in a province, it was never enough to cause much more than a disgruntled complaint that typically resulted in a royal visit from a low level royal to appease the faction.

Kahlahnni watched the steady stream of people; some walked, others rode, and several had a covered wagon or small cart. She settled against a tree trunk and tried to relax her mind, attempting to push away the heavy emotions that tried to cling to her, to invade her space. If she was honest with herself, she was a little scared she was not going to be able to ever get this under control and she would have to live by herself, a recluse for the remainder of her life. What had started off as seeing glimpses of people's lives or futures and being able to sense danger had now become more. She didn't know what had changed, whether it was the branding or the infection that had made an impact and changed her power. It may not have been either of those things, she just didn't know, but what she was learning was that all these negative emotions were making her feel ill, weak, and drained.

She normally hunched her shoulders to be less noticeable but now she hunched because what she felt was heavy, almost too heavy to carry. So many nasty, vile, sad, vulnerable thoughts warred with each other for dominance and she struggled to keep them at bay. Kahlahnni closed her eyes and a memory rose, a soft humming played in the back of her mind and she joined in without recognizing the tune. She just knew it. As she hummed what she would describe as a lullaby, the intrusion of outside emotions faded and a peace settled over her. With a sense of wonder, Lahnni stopped humming for a few moments and to her shock, the outside feelings began to creep in, she quickly started the tune again and the heaviness lifted. She smiled to herself and opened her eyes, the sinister, unhappy emotions returned, but not quite as strong, quickly she closed her eyes and her equilibrium of peace returned. It appeared that the humming and closed eyes combined worked the best, and the humming alone minimized it. Lahnni almost cried with relief.

The sun lost some of its heat as it dipped toward the horizon and Lahnni began to wonder how much longer Evan would be. She opened her eyes and swallowed against the now present heaviness and stood and stretched. She walked around slowly, getting circulation to return to her limbs, and through the trees spotted a sparkling surface. Fascinated, she walked to the edge of the trees and was greeted with a beautiful vista of a sloping hill running down to greet a wide winding river that sparkled with the afternoon sunlight. There were things on the river and she was fascinated by them, but too far away to see them clearly enough. She would have to ask Evan what they were when he got back.

"Excuse me?" a voice spoke behind her, clearing his throat as he spoke.

She jumped and spun in fright, her humming forgotten and at once the emotions of the people of Pessac washed over her. She smiled faintly at him and attempted to pretend that she was fine. "Hello." It was only now did she recognize the clothing the young man wore, it was very similar to what Evan had been wearing while they traveled, but this man wore no bonded circlets on his sleeves. This man of about twenty was a Roamer, a Pomaikka.

"Mother sent me to find out if you needed anything."

Kahlahnni wasn't concentrating on his words, she was staring at his face. His dark, thick wavy hair, his strong nose, and deep brown eyes. His skin was the same color as hers and he didn't tower over her, he was just a few inches taller. No more than five foot nine inches. She wanted to cry, to laugh, to yell. So many emotions coursed through her and most of them were her own. Until this moment she realized there had still been a hint of doubt that there was someone else like her, but here he was. Her own kind.

He watched her expectantly and she realized she needed to answer him. "My horse is skittish around too many people, so my bonded has gone into the city for supplies while I wait here." She didn't want to say more, though he looked the same as her it didn't mean she could trust him. Life had taught her too many times that most people only cared for themselves and what they could get from you.

"So, you don't need anything?" he asked again.

"Thank you, but no."

The Roamer shrugged his shoulders. He bowed his head slightly. "May your path be clear."

"Thank you." Lahnni smiled, uncertain at what the words meant.

The young man frowned and paused for a moment, his eyes flicked to her wrist before he turned and walked away. She watched him walk to the road and join a group of people wearing dark clothing. As she watched his back, she thought about his frown and suddenly realized that what he had said was probably something Pomaikka said to each other and there was almost certainly a response other than thank you. That's why he had looked to her wrist to make sure she wore the brand. Lahnni's jubilation waned as she realized even though she may have met someone that looked the same as her, she still didn't belong.

Kahlahnni continued to hum as they rode around the outside of the wall. She had quickly explained to Evannderth what she had discovered when he returned and he had asked to hear the song. After her humming to him, he had declared he had never heard it before, but it was a beautifully simple tune. For some inexplicable reason, his approval of the song made her happy. She had told him of the encounter with her first Roamer and had asked if he knew the response she was supposed to give to, "May your path be clear."

Evan had nodded and responded with, "And your life long."

"Is it something most people would know?"

"Not really. Only those that spend a lot of time with Roamers or who are Roamers."

"I didn't realize you had spent so much time with them."

"Not that much really, but if I am going to play the role of a bonded man then I better know the basics."

It stung to think he had played the role of someone else's bonded. It took all her self-restraint to not comment. Instead, she changed the subject. "Did you find out anything?"

"Here." He dug in the bag he carried and handed her an orange.

"Thank you."

"We are in luck. A troop of performers have a large tent set up on the other side of the city, near the river, as it's easier for their animals. We shall head there now, if you think you can handle the people? There will be many people there and around the area as they visit the carnival. Or we could wait here a little longer and hopefully by the time we arrive the performance will be over and the audience is on its way home."

"That sounds like it might work."

So, they had waited until the sun kissed the horizon and as they admired the pink skyline they mounted up and set out for the other side of the city. They gave it a wide berth to keep the emotions seeping out to find Lahnni to a manageable level. Thankfully the sky was clear and the moon full, making it easier to see.

As they turned the final corner and an enormous tent came into view, Lahnni panicked. There were people everywhere, streaming out of the wide open flaps and heading back into the city. She pulled her horse up short, humming loudly in an attempt to counteract the crowd before her when she realized that nothing heavy was butting against her. Kahlahnni stopped humming for a moment and smiled with amazement as kind, happy, cheerful feelings washed over her. They didn't cling like the negative; they made her feel light and free. All these people had enjoyed themselves and were exuding positivity as they left the carnival. It was a beautiful moment and one she would never forget.

With a smile on her face, she felt freer and not afraid to show it. These people weren't afraid of her or her kind. With that thought clear in her mind, she nudged her horse forward and Lahnni followed Evan into the Roamer camp area.

They were quickly approached by a middle-aged woman, who to Lahnni was gorgeous in a mysterious way.

Her dark hair was twisted up in a messy bun, her brown eyes glittered in the night light, and hard lacquered bangles in blue clicked against each other as she moved her hands while she talked. She had no bands around her vest or skirt, just beautiful patterns of flowers embroidered in yellow and blues on her vest. "Greetings to you."

"Hello," Evan answered. They had thought it best if he did the talking until they knew a little more. "I was hoping to speak to someone in charge about some training for my friend?"

The woman raised her eyebrows. "You are not bonded?"

"No. There are things I don't wish to explain here. My friend needs to learn your ways, she is newly branded and in need of guidance."

"She is Pomaikka, how does she not know our ways?"

"Another thing I do not wish to discuss out here. Is there no way I can speak to someone who makes these decisions?" Evan was calm, his demeanor pleasant.

"At the moment, you talk to me," she answered, waving her hands dismissively while her bangles clinked together.

He nodded his head in deferment.

The woman looked from Evan to Lahnni and stared at her for several moments. "Show me your brand," she ordered firmly.

Kahlahnni held out her hand, wrist up. The Roamer stepped forward and before Lahnni could react the woman grasped her hand and ran her thumb over the now healed, but still tender brand. Images of laughing children, prancing dogs, and a whispering of something unfathomable came to the surface of Lahnni's mind.

The Pomaikka dropped her hand like it was on fire and took several steps backward. Lahnni could feel the alarm radiating from the stranger. What had happened?

"She doesn't belong here," she said bluntly and Lahnni felt her hopes fade. Even her own kind didn't want her. She truly didn't belong.

"She is clearly a Roamer, one of the Pomaikka. Her brand is different, but not so different that it should cause you to behave this way," insisted Evan.

"Leave before I have you removed. You should know what will happen if you break peace with us," she warned.

"We will leave, but I will spread wide and far your lack of hospitality and your unwillingness to aid one of your own kind." Evan smiled pleasantly down at her.

"You do not know what you speak of," she warned.

"You do not know who you speak to," he countered.

Her face looked slightly worried but she held her ground.

Lahnni finally found her voice. "It is fine. I did not mean to cause trouble. We will leave." She turned her horse before either of them could see her tears. The happy feelings that came from the carnival goers had evaporated and she was again left with an empty ache that was slowly being fed negative energy coming from behind the city walls and now internally too. She truly was a freak that no one wanted.

Tears blurred her vision as the horrid emotions of people began to invade, she wanted to hum, to push it away but what was the point? Maybe she should let all the hatred and sadness in and let it take her. She was so intent on her misery that she almost missed the young man signaling to her to follow him. It was the same young man that had approached her this afternoon. He walked slowly amongst the other people and from her higher vantage point on her horse it was easy to follow him. She didn't look back to see if Evan followed, she didn't want to risk losing sight of the man.

Without conscious thought, she began to hum softly, keeping the powerful negative emotions of others to a minimum as she was still mostly surrounded by happy people. She realized that her thoughts must also influence what she took in. It was something to think about.

As she followed the young Roamer she realized they were heading toward the river. The crowd was starting to thin out but there were still plenty of people wanting to continue their merriment. They reached a landing where many long, flat boats with low cabins were lined up. They all had different symbols that she couldn't make out painted on their hull, but the boats all felt uniform in their appearance. The young man came to a halt and stood beside an older gentleman and an ancient-looking woman. There were fewer people around the area.

She dismounted as Evan came up next to her and then also dismounted. He gave her a quizzical look but didn't interfere with what she was doing. He trusted her and it made her feel stronger and more sure of herself.

"Hello again." She smiled at the man.

"May I see your brand?" the elder woman asked, cutting through the small talk.

Lahnni was hesitant after what had just happened at the Roamer camp, but how could she refuse this elderly Pomaikka? Kahlahnni held out her left hand, wrist up, and all three of them crowded around her, but none grabbed her arm. "May I touch it?" the gentleman asked.

"Yes." She braced for the images that would surely flood in, but instead, as the man took her hand and ran his fingers over the brand she got a sensation of relief, gratitude, and something like awe. It was very confusing.

As he let her arm go gently, he nodded to both the younger man and older woman, and without warning, all three dropped to their knees. "What are you doing?" Kahlahnni exclaimed.

"There have been signs for many moons that one with the gifts of old had been birthed, but you have remained hidden until a few weeks ago. We have been waiting for you." The old woman spoke rapidly. "We will take you and train you in not only the ways of the Pomaikka but also train your power so you can control it and use it."

Lahnni's mind reeled with the words and the meaning she felt behind them. There was no falsehood, just a want and desire to help and serve. "Please stand up." Kahlahnni moved to help the ancient woman up and was waved away.

The two men came to her aid and helped her to her feet. "I have nothing to hide but you are not ready to experience my mind," she explained.

Evan cleared his throat and everyone turned to look at him. "The Land Roamers didn't want to help her. The woman was extremely rude. I am used to a friendly level of hospitality when being around Pomaikka. Why would you help her?"

"Pfft." The woman dismissed his complaints. "She is not allowed to welcome the girl and give her hearth placement. That brand marks her as different and most would not know in what way but only that they must be declined hearth placement until they find their instructor. It has been two generations since that brand appeared and most think it only a myth, but they follow the laws of the old ways."

Evan nodded. "I will speak alone with my friend. Will you excuse us?"

The three Roamers withdrew a short distance.

"What do you want to do?" Evan asked Lahnni. She always liked how he didn't assume anything; he gave her choices. No one else had.

"I get only truth from what they are saying. They are truly happy to find me and help me," she explained. "I think I should go with them."

As sad as she had been for not knowing the ways of the Pomaikka, she was excited to find someone who would teach her. She would finally find her place and belong. The thought was intoxicating. But while she couldn't wait to begin her new life, she was sad to part ways with Evannderth. He had shown her that she needn't be afraid of everyone. Some people were good and wanted to help. And quietly in the far back of her mind and a large part of her heart, she admitted only to herself that she had fallen in love with him. She dreamed about him when she slept and thought about him constantly while she was awake, and daydreamed about him holding her and kissing her when she watched him while he was busy doing a task. Evan had become almost an obsession, and Lahnni knew that it was for the best to part ways with him before she made a fool of herself and tried to do something silly like flirt with him. He was older and probably interested in women who knew what they were doing and were far prettier than her and her Roamer appearance. She was young and naive and he had to rescue her so many times; had to care for her, feed her, and bathe her while she healed. None of that she figured was very romantic. "Thank you for everything you have done for me." She took in his beautiful eyes one more time, hoping to burn the memory of them into her mind to hold onto forever.

His voice was husky when he answered. "You are unique, never let anyone forget it, especially yourself. You long to fit in, but I hope one day you come to understand that it is more important to be you."

Kahlahnni felt pride, sadness, and something she couldn't articulate coming from him as she smiled sadly up at him. "I hope to meet you again someday." Her words were soft.

"I look forward to that day."

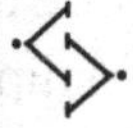

Evannderth

Kahlahnni's horse shook its head as if it didn't under-stand why the lovely girl that had been riding it was walking away without her. "I feel the same way, buddy." Evan spoke quietly to the horse as he tightened his grip on the reins.

Evan tried to ignore the lump that was forming in his throat as the gorgeous girl he had been pretending to be bonded to walked onto the gangplank of the longboat, and with one final wave, disappeared into the cabin and from his view. He swallowed around the hard lump and pushed away thoughts of chasing after her and admitting that he had fallen in love with her and that he had spent the entire time knowingly radiating warmth and kindness rather than the lust and longing he had felt. From the moment he had seen her brand he had known that she carried the gifts of old; after all, that was his job to know all the brands, including the rarest one.

With one final look at the closed cabin door, Evan mounted his horse and with Lahnni's horse in tow, headed into the city. Evan moved amongst the citizens of Pessac, occasionally getting jostled by the crowd as they went home, still chatting excitedly about the wonderful show the Roamers had put on or heading out for more entertainment as they wanted to continue the merriment. He liked the fact that he blended in with the crowd today and was able to hear snippets of everyday conversation rather than guarded ones he typically overheard when he was in uniform. That reminded him that he needed to pick up a completely new set of uniforms. He put that at the top of the list he needed to accomplish.

I need to report in and have messages sent that the troop will need a new sergeant and another private. I need to fill out an incident report regarding Ambrosse. He made a list in his head. *Once that is done I need to get back to the Twin Cities and report in. Some people will need to know the truth about Ambrosse and add it to the growing concerns of why the branding ceremony is choosing people not suitable for their brands. It is baffling, but someone else's problem,* he reminded himself. *You need to be concerned about getting back to her and setting up a network to keep a watch on Kahlahnni until she is trained. There is still much to be done and the newborn prince must be protected.*

And with all those whirling thoughts in his head, Evannderth put his feelings for Lahnni aside and refocused on the cause he had pledged his life to many years ago.

Chapter 11

Part Two

Evannderth

The long boat had been moored for several turnings, and still no one had left it or even come up on deck. He was becoming impatient. All his informants had told him that this was her boat and the black feather painted on the side of the stern would indicate that it was true. He remembered how she had treasured the black feather she found while they were in the forest on the way to Pessac. It reminded her of freedom. It was dusk and the last rays of the sun cast long shadows across the wide river. The tall double towers of the Brothers of Seggar that sat on the opposite side of the river in the city of Arsenny looked ominous in the darkening sky. They were large and bulky, made from mismatched blocks of blue stone. Evan had always preferred the Sisters of Seggar double towers, with their thinner, more spire-like appearance, carved from sandstone. They sat in the city of Csennia, twin to Arsenny, and the one he currently called home.

Evan drained the dregs of his tankard and went to order another when he stopped raising his arm in mid-motion. The cabin door had opened. He waved away the bar wench who was about to approach, and placed a few coins on the table. It had begun to drizzle outside, which gave him the perfect excuse to pull his hood up and cover his face. He stood under the awning of the rundown tavern and watched with wonder as the woman who filled his dreams stood in the doorway to the longboat cabin. He only managed to get a glimpse of her perfect features before she pulled on a cloak and covered her face with a hood.

He was surprised to find his heart racing and a fire slowly lighting in his lower belly. Even after four years she still managed to have this effect on him. If he wasn't careful this could get messy. He had a job to do and it wasn't bedding that gorgeous Pomaikka. As she moved across the short gangplank to the low pier, Evan practiced his breathing techniques he learned a long time ago, and settled his mind, telling himself that he felt nothing but friendship for the girl and that he had to project non-threatening calmness just like last time. She must continue to trust him.

The young man that talked to her under the tree all those years ago and had recognized her different brand and had brought her to his family followed her. He watched her with adoring eyes and Evan felt a surge of jealousy, which he quickly dampened. She always felt negative emotions more strongly.

Evan kept his head down and bent to adjust his boot as she walked by. As he straightened, he watched with awe at the way she held herself. Gone were the hunched shoulders and lowered gaze. She met the world face on, her head held high. Her cloak gave off an odd sheen in the light rain and he wondered what it was made from. He listened to her heels click on the uneven cobblestones of the street as he followed her into the richer merchant district.

The streets were full as people made their way home from work or hurried to a dinner engagement. Couples strolled along the wider boulevards, most heading toward the central market square of the area where there was a troupe of Roamers that had been performing for the past week. There had been rumors circulating that the famous fortune teller, Kahlahnni Pomaikka, would be arriving in the city for her first visit and when it had reached Evan's spy network he put his final plan into action in case it was true.

Though Kahlahnni was shorter than most, she had a presence to her that instantly made people give way and move aside. This made it easier to follow her, though he did have an idea where she would end up. There had been several canopies of varying sizes set up in the central market of the merchants' sector for the performers to entertain under with the inclement weather that always happened around this time of year.

He watched as she was greeted by several Roamers with deep courteous bows and shown to a small canopied area that held a tiny square table and two chairs, one on either side. She was shown to a chair and the young man who had escorted her spoke to someone who nodded and hurried away. He then took up a position behind Kahlahnni and crossed his arms, scowling at anyone who stood too close.

Under the shelter of the open tent, Kahlahnni no longer needed the hood and pulled it back from her face. Evan smiled to himself as he caught glimpses of her through the gathering crowd. She was magnificent. She pulled her rich, dark brown hair out from the cloak and settled its beautiful curls around her shoulders. He allowed himself a moment of lust, letting a stray thought of the idea of running his fingers through her hair come to mind. He imagined Kahlahnni on top of him, leaning over as she rode him, her hair trailing along his chest as she bent to kiss him. He grew hard with the idea and was grateful for the heavy soldier cloak he wore. There would be more than his lustful emotions for her to deal with at the moment, so he felt safe in not keeping his thoughts neutral and pleasant.

The crowd grew silent as her first client sat across from her. She dramatically removed her velvet gloves and laid them on the table next to her. Evan moved closer to see if he could hear what was being said. His rank displayed clearly on his cloak made people stand aside when they usually wouldn't, he didn't need to move too close, his height gave him an advantage.

"Give me your hands," he heard her say and watched her hold hers out.

The man, in what Evan guessed was his mid-thirties, took her hands, showing no sign of hesitancy.

"Ask your question."

"Will I get what I desire?"

Evan was disappointed. *That's extremely vague,* he thought to himself. Was the guy a plant to lull people into spending their money?

Kahlahnni sat there for several moments before she closed her eyes. "Your question should have been what do you desire. You are at a crossroads. You can attain your greatest desire, but you need to understand what that is or you will never appreciate it."

The man frowned. "I don't understand."

Kahlahnni opened her eyes and let go of his hands, she sighed heavily. Evan smiled at the drama of it. "I doubt you will understand until you let go of your childish wants. Be a man; seek your truth."

A young Roamer girl hurried over with a gold goblet and matching ewer. She placed them both on the table and bowed. Kahlahnni poured herself a drink and waited for the man to leave and someone new to take his seat. Evan surmised that as there seemed to be no money changing hands that the arrangements had all been done prior and this spectacle was for the benefit of gaining more clients when she returned. The man was replaced by a heavily pregnant woman.

"Give me your hands," Kahlahnni said, her voice less brisk.

With shaking hands the young woman reached out. Even from this distance, Evan could make out the red, raw hands of someone that did hard work with liquids of some kind. They joined hands and this time Kahlahnni closed her eyes immediately. She didn't ask her to ask a question, she just sat there holding the woman's hands. The crowd grew solemn as they waited for what would happen. *Her showmanship is a definite wonder,* he thought sarcastically as the tension built. Kahlahnni opened her eyes and leaned forward and spoke quietly to the pregnant woman. The woman wailed loudly, clear pain in her cries, but Kahlahnni kept a grip on her hands and continued to whisper. Evan rolled his eyes at the melodrama and quickly regretted his snide thoughts when a whisper reached him that the woman had just been informed that the babe she carried was gone, just like two previous pregnancies. Then a second whisper spread that she had been told to stop working at the tannery while pregnant, for there would be another baby, and this one would live if she did what she was told.

For the next turning, Kahlahnni told various people riddles that they would need to decipher like the first man she had seen or clear advice like the pregnant woman. Some she asked what they wanted to know, others she told what she felt they needed to hear. He hoped she would be able to help him.

Once it was announced that Kahlahnni was done for the evening, but that she would be back in two nights and she still had a few appointments left for those that wanted them, the crowd began to disperse while a few stayed to see if they could be seen. She didn't linger, rather she stood and pulled the hood of her strange cloak over her head, leaving the young man to take questions while she walked out into the square and moved into the crowd. Evan followed her, having to push past several people to keep up. She hurried out of the square and turned down a road; Evan quickened his steps to keep her in sight and as he turned the corner he ran into a figure.

Rich brown eyes glared up at him. "What do you want?" she demanded.

He struggled not to lose control of his emotions and reveal his feelings as he longed to succumb to her glorious eyes and kiss her upturned mouth. Instead, Evan pulled back his hood and smiled softly at her. "Hi, Lahnni."

Kahlahnni

That voice, those aquamarine eyes. Her heart thudded against her chest and for a second she was in a cave, her ankle ruined, her brand infected, her knees scraped, her head cut, and starving, but with him there she was safe. "Evan." She uttered his name without realizing it.

"I am sorry if I frightened you. I was trying to catch you to ask you if you had time to have a drink with an old friend."

Kahlahnni sensed that there was more, but didn't let down her shields to discover what. She allowed him his privacy. Her stomach fluttered as she looked up at him. "I would love to have a drink with you. Where would you like to go?"

"There is a place back in the market that should be suitable and you won't be bothered."

"Lead the way."

Evan turned around and headed back to the large market square. There was still plenty of people around as many Roamer performers were still about while others peddled their wares. He led her to a small establishment that had bright light spilling from the window and a quiet atmosphere as they entered. "A private dining room, please," Evan asked as he entered.

They were ushered up to a second floor and shown into a small room with a cloth covered round table and two thickly padded chairs. "Someone will be here shortly to take your order. The kitchen is still open if you require food," the friendly matron said as she closed the door behind her.

"Let me take your cloak." Evan held out his hands and Kahlahnni turned, unclasping the top as she did.

"Be careful with it. It was a gift."

She turned back to find him staring at it. He looked up in wonder. "It's made of feathers."

"The outer layer is. It keeps the water off, just like it would a bird." She watched him turn an edge and look at the lining. "It's the same shiny material your shirts are made from."

"Yes."

He took great care as he hung it on a hook by the door before he removed his cloak. "What type of bird is it from? The feathers are so black and glossy."

"I am told they are from a black swan." She didn't want to talk about feathers at the moment, she wanted to stand and admire him in his uniform. He looked the same as he did the day he had rescued her.

"You always did have a thing for feathers. The gift suits you."

"Thank you."

"Sit, be comfortable. Tell me about yourself. I managed to catch part of your readings and am fascinated."

Lahnni laughed. "I don't think I have ever heard you so eager before. Where is the calm, level-headed soldier that rescued me?"

"Oh, I'm still here. I just don't need to be as quiet around you now. I get the feeling you don't scare as easily anymore. After all, you just confronted me on the street," he pointed out.

She pursed her lips. "True." Lahnni settled into the chair he held out for her. "I was frightened of everything back then."

"With good reason," he pointed out kindly. "You did not have a great start to life. Not knowing who you were, and never belonging, and always being treated differently." Evan took a seat and smiled at her. "But now look at you. You have found your place. You belong. You are a Roamer."

"I don't fit in anymore with the Pomaikka than I did in the town of Gennestenmont. I am either shunned or worshiped, but never just accepted for me. Some fear me and others covet my abilities. It is not what I expected." It was hard for her to admit, and she wasn't sure why she was telling this to a man that she had known for barely a month over four years ago.

There was a polite knock on the door and a young girl came in and curtsied quickly before asking them what they would like to drink. "A flagon of your best red, please," Lahnni answered. "What is there hot to eat?"

"There is half a venison pie left."

"Two slices please."

The girl looked to Evan who shook his head. She curtsied again and left the room.

Silence filled the room and Lahnni began to regret her outburst. She had made Evan feel uncomfortable. Just because she thought of him as her safe space didn't mean he thought of her in any way other than a supplicant who had become a complication. "So, you are no longer out running the branding ceremonies in the provinces?" She tried to fill the void with a question.

"No. I was recalled after delivering you to the Roamers."

"I hope I had nothing to do with it?" She tried not to think about Ambrosse and she didn't bring up his name.

"Not at all. I was recommended for a role in court, so have been doing that." Evan frowned at her. "I thought you said you could feel their sincerity. That you trusted them."

"They are both. But they also treat me like I am a gift from the Gods rather than just another Roamer. It is unsettling and comes with a lot of pressure. People don't always like the answers they seek and take it out on me."

He nodded at her. "That's why some of your answers were vague. You didn't want to deal with how they would react to the whole truth."

"I also can't see everything. Some are clear and easy to read. Others are hidden and that's when I ask questions to get them to think about what they want to know."

"So you do more than feel their emotions now?"

"I occasionally get a glimpse of something. It comes to me in pictures." She was beginning to understand that her abilities fluctuated and sometimes only half the truth was revealed. It was more than likely because the person she was reading had not made up their mind yet. Once their path was clear, she could read it better. "What I have learned to do is shield. I can block out most of what people project."

"That's great. I always worried that you would never be able to be around too many people. And now look at you, in the middle of the Twin cities, looking beautiful, calm, and totally in control of yourself."

Lahnni flushed at the word beautiful. A polite knock interrupted their conversation as the young girl returned with two older teens carrying their food and drink. They left as quietly and efficiently as they arrived.

As they both ate their pie and drank their wine they exchanged light-hearted tales of their lives over the last four years.

"I have been to the settlement," Lahnni told him between bites of the spicy pie. "The fabled city of the Pomaikka." She dropped her voice and leaned forward. "You were right. There is so much going on there. So many secrets," she teased.

"Oh, come on. You have to tell me something. You can't just leave it like that."

"Only if you tell me something about you. I know nothing about you."

Evan grinned at her. "You could just read me."

"That would be rude. And all I ever get from you is competence and calm," Lahnni admitted.

"Are you sure there is nothing else?"

Lahnni tilted her head to one side and studied him before she settled into her seat a little further, breathed out, and inch by inch drew her shield into her core. Thoughts, emotions, and images tried to batter at her, but she was more experienced and little frightened her anymore. She had witnessed the worst of humanity through their eyes and she pitied them. Kahlahnni looked at Evannderth for several more minutes; she noted the subtle tightness around his body, particularly his shoulders and jawline. "You want to ask me something, but are holding back." With those words she took several breaths before pushing outwards with her mind, creating a shield around herself again. Shutting the world down to a dull, listless murmur. She looked at him and waited.

He raised his blond eyebrows at her. "Impressive."

"What do you want to ask me?"

"I came looking for you to see you, but also because I have a friend who would love to have a reading but can't go out and have one in public."

Lahnni thought about what he had said before and came to a quick conclusion. "You want me to meet the royal you work for?"

"You are clever. Yes, I do." Evan took the final bite of his pie and waited for her to answer.

She took her time chewing and thought about seeing a royal. This was someone with power. Lahnni didn't need trouble and she also didn't want them knowing too much about her abilities. It was another reason for the sometimes cryptic answers. She had to look like she was covering up possibilities and second guessing herself. She finished her goblet of red and poured another. "I'm not sure if that is a good idea, Evan."

"It would mean a lot to me, and I will keep you safe. She just wants a reading like anyone else."

"Who do you work for?"

"Lady Darria."

Kahlahnni knew her face showed shock. "The old queen?"

"We don't use that phrase around her. Obviously a touchy subject."

"I imagine it would be. Nothing like getting cast aside for your younger sister when you don't produce an heir. And then it is rumored to keep up your dalliances with the King, your now ex-husband, while your sister produces two heirs."

Evan nodded. "That about sums it up." He finished his drink and poured another. "She hasn't told me, but she is keeping a secret, and from the hints she is dropping it is significant."

Lahnni had a bad feeling. Something was not sitting right, but she couldn't fathom what it was. She didn't want to do a reading for any member of the royal family, especially such a controversial one, but she knew she could not say no. This is what she had been trained for. What Kahlahnni had not told Evannderth while she spoke about the fabled settlement of Pomaikka was that she had been given some basic training as a spy and been told that while she was traveling she was to take every and all opportunities to gather information when it presented itself for the King of Segarris, whom the Roamers served.

"Finish your drink and take me to see your friend. Though I am a little disappointed to learn that you didn't come looking for me just to see how I was." She said it lightly, but hoped he could feel the truth underneath.

Evan had the grace to blush and while the young, naive Lahnni would have been at a loss at what to do, the more mature and seasoned Kahlahnni smiled sweetly and arched an eyebrow at him.

Chapter 12

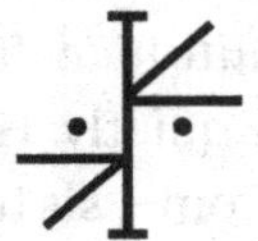

"Lady Darria, may I present Kahlahnni of the Po-maikka." Evannderth spoke the words formally.

Lahnni did as she had been instructed and curtsied. She let her shields down a fraction and felt nothing but curiosity and eagerness from the former queen. Lahnni hardened her emotional shield, relieved that Lady Darria appeared to be what Evan claimed. She felt something off, but maybe it was just that she had had too many red wines and was slightly tipsy and not as focused as normal, as her mind kept wandering back to the man standing beside her. It seemed that Evan still had her heart.

"It is a pleasure to meet you, my dear."

"I am honored," Kahlahnni responded, not quite knowing what else to say.

"I hope you don't mind me using your friendship with Captain Evannderth to coerce you into doing a reading for me." Lady Darria spoke the words, but Lahnni didn't get the impression she meant them.

"Not at all. I do understand your want for privacy." Lahnni smiled. "Though, I am not sure how much help I will be." She looked to Evan. "I fear the Captain may have exaggerated my abilities. Much of what I do is read people's body language, clothing, and a few other tells that make me appear gifted in ways I am not."

Lady Darria pouted. *She probably thinks she looks slightly put out, Lahnni thought. But there is a sullenness and hardness she can't quite hide.* "Let us hope the Captain was right," Darria spoke quietly. Her voice brightened as she smiled at Lahnni. "Come, sit here with me."

Lahnni allowed herself to be led to a table that held four chairs. The chairs were padded and covered in plush brown fabric that reminded Kahlahnni of Lady Aisllyn, the elderly woman she had served so many years ago. The small personal sitting room of Lady Darria was tastefully decorated in browns with the occasional highlight of green and gold. Lit candelabra chased any shadows away on this drizzly night and thick fur-lined rugs kept the chill from the slate floor to a minimum. She took a seat and waited.

The older woman took the seat opposite and looked at Kahlahnni expectantly. "Now what?" she asked.

Keeping her nerves under control, Kahlahnni placed her hands, palm up, on the table. "Give me your hands," she said, trying to pretend this important woman was just like anyone else.

Lady Darria did what she was told. Lahnni noted that she wore a wedding band on her left hand. Lahnni sat still, concentrating on her heart beating to set a rhythm and focus point. And as shown by the man that trained the suspected assassins of Pomaikka, Kahlahnni found her center and slowed her breathing until she controlled her mind completely. No random thoughts could enter, only those she allowed in. She felt the touch of Lady Darria and the images that pushed against her shields, wanting to be witnessed. With great care, Lahnni opened the channel that allowed her control over how much she saw.

"Do you have a question?"

"I have many."

"I can only see what I see," warned Lahnni.

"What do you see then?"

The image formed slowly. Darria stood on a raised dais, a branding symbol burned behind her. It flickered between two different symbols. A powerfully built, tall man with a lined face and white close-cropped beard stood to one side, he wore a gold and silver woven circlet. Lahnni assumed this man was King Tommofey, Lady Darria's husband, until she had been cast aside for being barren. A fine mist connected the King to the Lady and she stood there, her hands covering her belly. She watched the sun rise and fall and the Lady's belly grow until in the moment between blinks she held a naked baby boy in her arms.

Kahlahnni opened her eyes and hesitated, she looked at Darria then at the two guards that stood on either side of her door, and at Evannderth, who stood nearby. "Are you certain you want all to hear what I have to say?"

"Wait outside," she ordered the two guards. "Captain, you may stay."

They waited until the bodyguards closed the door soundly behind them and then both Darria and Evan turned back to watch her expectantly. "You carry the King's son," Kahlahnni spoke bluntly, her feelings of danger grew as she spoke. "He will be born healthy and whole." She withdrew her hands.

Lady Darria covered her belly with a hand. "Good. That is what I wanted to know." She sat back in her chair.

"Would you care for some tea? I find it is the only thing that does not make me feel ill at the moment."

"Tea would be lovely," answered Kahlanni when what she wanted to ask was for permission to leave and have Evan take her from here and find another private room where she could spend more time with him.

"Captain, please have a servant send up some of my herbal tea, and then find me a Brother of the Seggar, who can come and bear witness that a seer who wears the old brand of the Pomaikka says that the child I carry is the King's."

Evan looked concerned. For the first time since Lahnni had known him did she feel anything other than calm from him. Even when they were being attacked by four men did he radiate nothing but confidence, at the moment what she felt was a mixture of emotions all tumbling onto each other—all too quick to recognize anyone. What was he hiding? "I will be back with the Priest soon." He said it more to Kahlahnni than to Lady Darria.

"No need. Just send him over. I will make certain Kahlahnni is returned to her people once I am finished with her."

Kahlahnni didn't like the feeling that came with those words and opened herself up a little more to the emotions in the room. What she felt from the Lady was determination and a clear intent to get her way. Perhaps if Lahnni just went along with it, it would be over soon. After all, this was not the first time she had had to deal with a too demanding client. She was adept at misdirection and half-truths. "It is fine," she told Evan. What she wanted to add was that she hoped to see him again soon, but didn't dare while in the company of Darria.

"See? Now, run along."

Evan looked again at Lahnni, who gave him an encouraging smile that she didn't feel before he bowed to both of them and left the room. As soon as the door closed, the tall older woman, who Lahnni guessed was nearing her forties, sat forward and clasped her hand without permission. "I want to know it all. I want to know who will rule? My son will have the right to rule, but will he?"

Powerful images forced their way into Lahnni's mind. It was difficult to block someone out when they had physical contact and focused all their thought on what they wanted. This time the royal dais was crowded. Lady Darria stood proudly next to a grown man with light brown hair and hazel eyes.

On the other side of the dais stood another woman, she was marginally fairer in coloring than Darria, but it was easy to see the resemblance of her sister, Queen Anzhellika. Beside her stood two men, both tall, one in royal finery, one in the deep blue of the Brother's of Seggar. Between the sisters and what Lahnni assumed were their grown sons was the state robes of the King, in a crumpled heap with the metal woven crown resting upon it and beside it a set of scales. The same branding symbol hovered above the scene, changing from one symbol to another, then back again. A dark orb sat in the front of Lady Darria and her son, it flashed with lightning strikes and cries of battle seemed to emanate from it. A brighter orb sat at the foot of Queen Anzhellika and her sons, it seemed to contain sunlight, but a pool of blood sat in its center. On either side flickered flimsy images of two specters, but neither was clear other than she could tell their general human shape.

There was so much to take in in the scene and most of it she didn't understand. As Lahnni refocused her efforts and gained control of her shields, slowly building them, the image faded, but was replaced with a vague picture of a huge, round, stone structure with many levels that looked like stairs. Kahlahnni wrenched her hands from the tight grip of Darria and glowered at her as she shut down all emotions from being received.

"Tell me," the lady demanded, all pretense of manners gone.

Kahlahnni stalled for time as she collected her thoughts. She needed to be careful; there was more at play here than she understood and for some reason, she felt that she was somehow involved in it. How dare Evan bring her into this situation.

"I am not sure I can help you. All I see is your son standing upon the dais with you, he is a young man."

"Is he King?"

"It did not show me who was King," she said evasively, though technically she was not lying.

Darria's eyes narrowed, but before she could say more there was a knock on the door. "That will be our tea," she said brightly. "Come in."

They both sat quietly as a servant entered and prepared tea for both of them before quickly retreating. As the door was closed, Kahlahnni picked up the delicate cup with both hands so the Lady could not snatch at them again and try to force further answers. She took a sip, it was delicious.

"I am sorry that I can't see what you want me to see," Lahnni apologized, trying to smooth over the heated exchange.

"That's a shame," Lady Darria answered in a voice that made Lahnni feel nervous. What had Evan brought her into? "Your readings are told to be the most accurate in centuries. You carry the mark of the gifted, yet you can not give me what I want to know."

"Most of it is subterfuge," Lahnni tried to deflect. "People give off signs and tells about themselves all the time. I could guess you were pregnant by the King simply by the fact you continually cradle your stomach like many pregnant women and you still wear your wedding band, even though you are no longer wed to him. He would not allow that unless he still held you in great affection."

"Clever." Lady Darria smiled cruelly, her lips thinning into a snarl. "But I don't believe you. You hold people's hands because skin on skin contact gives you the clearest read. You can get clear feelings and emotions from being in close proximity or more general if there are a lot of people around. But the visions that always came with the brand you carry only happen through physical contact Evan tells me."

Kahlahnni's heart raced. Evan had told her most private secrets, he had shared what no one knew but a few in the upper circles of the Pomaikka. How could he? It was impossible to believe that the man she cared about so deeply had betrayed her. Her head felt funny and she was struggling to keep her emotions under control. *You're tired and not thinking straight*, she told herself. "I don't believe you."

Lady Darria leaned forward, her lips thinning further as her smile widened. Lahnni took another sip of her tea, pretending that this conversation wasn't bothering her. "Then tell me, my dear, has Captain Evannderth ever touched you with his bare hands?"

And with those words, Lahnni's world came crashing in.

Chapter 13

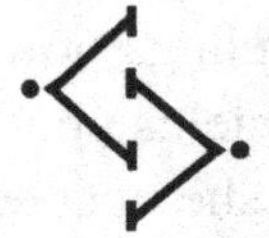

Kahlahnni woke lying on a strange bed. She whimpered in pain as the weight of all the emotions from the people of the Twin Cities of Arsenny and Csennia rolled over her. Negative, horrid thoughts pounded her while her mind spiraled as it tried to recall all the times Evannderth had touched her. The countless times he carried her to and from the river, he held her while she drank, he tended her wounds, cleaned her branding, every single one of them he had worn gloves.

He had always known what she was and how it worked and he had allowed her to struggle through without telling her anything. She had thought he was trustworthy, that he had truly cared about what happened to her. Now it seemed it had all been a plan to get her trained so he could bring her before the horrid woman he worked for to be used as a personal fortune teller. This had always been Kahlahnni and the Elder Roamer's greatest fear. That if people truly understood the value of her gift she could become a political pawn and her life would be in danger. *It's completely unfair that I can tell another's future but not my own. I am blinded to my own fate or to those that can affect it.*

She tried to sit up, but the pain was too much. It was like the dark feelings were holding her down. Why were her shields not in place? She had trained so hard and for so long for them to hold even while she slept. There were so many voices and feelings now that she couldn't find her own to bring her shields up.

It was terrifying and she needed it to stop.

Lying flat on her back, Kahlahnni looked at the fancy, light-colored material that hung over the top of her large bed. She moved her head and took in the wide room and the heavy curtains; she could see light around the edges of the window. She had been here all night.

Her mind raced as she tried to put together what had happened. The tea. Her mind had become foggy and she had found it difficult to concentrate. She had thought it was because she was upset about discovering Evannderth's bitter betrayal but it must have been the tea. The tea had somehow affected her ability to stay focused, which was causing her to not be able to shield, in turn allowing the overwhelming dark and disturbed emotions of the citizens of the Twin Cities to feed into her negative thought patterns creating more difficulties.

Stop! she yelled at herself within her head. *Focus. Go back to basics. Figure it out.* Kahlahnni closed her eyes and instead of fighting the bad feelings she allowed them in but did not hold onto them; instead she pushed them out again. She could hold onto her sanity for a while doing this. *At least long enough for you to figure out what to do next,* she told herself. *You need to move, you need to get out of here. Lady Darria wants to keep you as a pet. To help gain her son the throne.* Her mind screamed at her over the top of everything.

Lahnni's body was heavy; she focused on just moving one finger, one foot. Not big movements, only small ones. She just needed to hold on until the tea left her system and she had control back. Tears leaked from her eyes and she cried. A sob caught in her throat and she began to cough.

How could he do this to her?

You have to keep the negativity at bay; the more you think it, the more you attract it. Easier said than done. She scoffed at herself. Her mind circled back to Evan. There were so many questions. How did he know so much about her gift? What did he do for Lady Darria? Why would he help a woman like that?

Sadness and helplessness engulfed her and she felt small again. Vulnerable, like she had been as a child, never knowing her place. Never knowing who to trust and discovering that was no one. *You were wrong then and you are wrong now. People care about you, they always have. Just not always in a way you understood.*

Her stubborn streak reasserted itself and she gained minor control over her emotions. Enough that she could roll onto her stomach and slither to the end of the bed. Crying in frustration now, Lahnni slid off the bed, ending up in a crumpled heap on the floor. She waited and counted to ten to see if anyone came into her room. Nothing happened.

The heaviness of her limbs continued but she struggled against it. She would not be held captive, she was not a caged bird to be put on display and never freed. She thought of her black feather cloak and all it represented. *You are a beautiful black swan, accepted and admired. You may not belong anywhere but neither will you be forced to be somewhere ever again.*

With tears streaming down her face, her nose running from crying, and a profound sadness of betrayal from the one she trusted above all others, Lahnni crawled on all fours towards the door. She had no plan other than to reach it. *One thing at a time.*

As she crawled, she spotted her cloak draped over a divan in the corner. Be damned if she was leaving that behind. Kahlahnni changed direction and painstakingly made her way to the luxurious looking divan. She grabbed the bottom of the cloak and with every ounce of her being, tugged at it hard enough that it slid off the lounge and landed on her. Lahnni collapsed in a crumpled heap and breathed heavily for a few minutes.

As she did, she realized that her mind had cleared and the fogginess had lifted a little further. With a sigh of relief, she strengthened her weakened shield a little more and the weight of people lifted a fraction. Using the back of the long divan, Lahnni hauled herself up until she was standing.

The door banged open and Kahlahnni jumped with fright. She grasped the back of the couch harder; she would not let them see how badly affected she was. Her face hardened as she watched Evan enter the room. "What do you want?" her voice was cold.

"Lahnni..." he began, but she cut him off.

"Don't *Lahnni* me."

He stopped in front of her, his eyes sad as he looked at her. It was only then did she realize he could see that she had been crying. "I repeat: what do you want?" She couldn't feel anything from him, but now she understood he knew how to mask himself from her. She also was so flooded with others' emotions at the moment that unless she touched him it was hard to distinguish between him and everyone else. "Have you come to gloat?" She held up her hand, still holding the feather cloak. "Look at the prize you caught."

"Lahnni..." he tried again.

She glared at him.

"Kahlahnni." He spoke her name formally as if understanding she had rescinded his right to use the less formal name.

"Yes, Captain?" She spat out the words. "Have you come to command me to tell Lady Bitchface what I saw?"

"I have come to get you out of here, unless you would like to stand here and argue a little longer and possibly get caught?"

"How can I trust you?" Her voice broke.

"Do you have a choice?" His voice was kind and she hated it at that moment.

"Evannderth," she said softly, not wanting to say the next words but having no choice.

"Yes, Kahlahnni?"

"I can't walk. I think she poisoned me. My gifts aren't working."

"Then allow me to do what I have always done."

"And what is that?"

"Carry you."

Before she had time to protest, he moved forward and picked her up, cradling her against his solid body. A familiar calmness engulfed her and for the first time since she had woken, she could breathe properly without any heaviness on her chest.

"I need you to pretend you are asleep. Can you do that? There will be fewer questions if you can't answer them. If she has poisoned you then they will expect you to be asleep."

"I can do that. It is painful to be awake." Kahlahnni closed her eyes.

Evan began to hum the song that she had discovered could block out unwanted emotions all those years ago. Lahnni's eyes flew open and she stared up into his aquamarine ones; the eyes she fell in love with that had betrayed her. "How did you remember that?"

"I remember everything about you."

"Then why do this to me?" Lahnni muttered. She closed her eyes and slumped against him. She was too tired to demand more and she was still struggling to remain in control of herself.

"It's complicated."

"Hope it was worth it."

Evan began to hum again and some of the pressure eased; enough for her to settle against his chest and hang onto her sanity as he carried her out of the room. She closed her eyes and heard him explain that he was taking her to a room deeper in the palace as she needed to be hidden when people came looking for her. As she listened to his heartbeat and humming, she breathed in his scent and Lahnni found her mind finally settling and reasserting its natural barriers. She didn't know how he helped, but it was now obvious that he did. And with those final thoughts, she drifted off to sleep as he carried her through the castle, telling each person they met a different story. When it was finally discovered that she was gone, no one would be able to say for sure what he said as there would be so many conflicting versions, that people would begin to doubt themselves.

Chapter 14

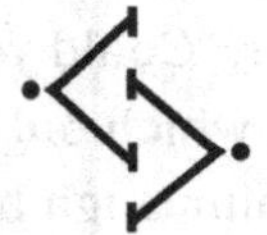

It had taken a full day of hiding in several dark, damp rooms and then an uncomfortable boat ride hidden in the cargo hold to cross the river into the city of Arsenny where the King and Queen of Segarris ruled, and where Lady Darria was not welcome, before Lahnni was laid down on a soft, clean bed and told to sleep by Evan.

As Kahlahnni came awake, she took stock of her internal senses. Her shields were back up, no more oppressive emotions weighing on her. She was safe behind her walls and was grateful to discover her mind fog had lifted. Lahnni rolled over and opened her eyes to find Evannderth sitting quietly by the darkened window. She took in her surroundings, her memory coming back and realized she was in the palace. The room was dark, only lit by a single candle that sat above an empty fireplace. The shadows told her that there was a table and chairs on one side of the fireplace, and on the other side was a long, low-shaped shadow that Lahnni couldn't quite make out.

She stared at Evan's profile for a moment, admiring his strong jaw and high forehead. "Why did you do it?" She spoke quietly.

He didn't jump, he just turned his head to look at her as she sat up. "There are things at play you don't understand," he said mysteriously.

She snorted at him as she rearranged the blanket that had been draped on her. "Could you be more cryptic?"

Evannderth laughed, which only made her deepen her scowl, in turn making him laugh harder.

"Really? That is all you are going to say? You take me out of the only place I feel safe, leave me to some power hungry maniac who wants to see her son gain the crown at all costs, tell her my secrets and abilities which I have spent my life hiding. You then burst in, claim I should still trust you, and take me away to another palace and another room I assume I can't leave."

He had stopped laughing about halfway through her speech. "Well, when you put it like that it doesn't sound great."

"You are still avoiding saying anything." Lahnni threw the blanket aside, too angry and restless to remain in bed, and stood. "I will not wait idly by for someone else to decide my fate. I don't trust you." To her surprise, her voice caught in her throat. "The Lady was right. I fooled myself or you fooled me into thinking you cared for me... I am not sure which one, maybe it was both. But now I know better and I am done playing games." She moved toward the door.

Evannderth leaped to his feet and beat her to the locked door. He blocked her path, his hands held up in front of him. "Please don't go."

"Why?" she demanded. "Are you really going to keep me prisoner here?"

He put his hands down. "No. If you want to leave I will let you, but your life is now in terrible danger because of me."

Lahnni took a step back and put her hands on her hips. "Do I detect a hint of guilt?" She said it out loud but knew that she was actually sensing it from him.

"Yes." He moved away from the door, indicating that if she wanted to leave he would not stop her. "I have put you in danger and for that I am sorry, but there is far more at stake than you think. I know I betrayed you." His voice had grown quiet. "I needed to know what Lady Darria was plotting and you were my key. I should have asked for your help, not just used you."

She looked at the face of the man she had dreamt about for years and felt confused. She had trusted him for so long and had told him things she had never told anyone else, only now to discover that he wasn't who she thought he was. As she had laid in that bed, when she could not move, held down by emotions and blocked from herself by the tea, the words of Lady Darria had kept repeating themselves.

Those words returned to her now.

"Tell me, my dear child, has he ever allowed you to touch him? To see his truth?"

Instead of asking him why, she chose to ask him something else. "Why have you not asked what I saw when I touched her?"

"I know what you saw. I was there, remember?" He looked confused.

"How do you know I told the truth?"

He began to laugh again. "You are magnificent."

Lahnni's demeanor softened slightly and she moved back to the bed and sat down. "I am?"

"Yes. Everyone underestimates you and I would do well to remember that."

"Does that everyone include you?" She didn't know why the answer was important.

"At times I have, but then you say something like that to remind me." He leaned forward on his chair. "Will you tell me all that you saw when she touched you?"

Lahnni also leaned forward and smiled at him. "No."

The room filled with silence as they stared at each other. Outside noises filtered in. People walking down corridors, she could hear voices laughing and someone else singing. The sounds of a palace filled with people all living their lives.

"I'm sorry." Evannderth finally broke the silence.

"For what?"

"For all the hurt I have caused you. For not confiding in you after you revealed everything to me."

"Darria asked if I had ever read you. She guessed that you had never allowed me to touch you as you knew how my gifts work." Lahnni drew in a sharp breath and looked down to the floor, too scared to see his face. "I was completely dumbfounded when I looked back and realized that it was true; you had never once allowed me to accidentally touch you. You always knew what I was and you always hid," she accused.

"Yes, but if you think about it you can also sense truth and you have never felt me tell you anything that wasn't true, have you?"

Kahalanni paused; she hadn't considered that. "I don't know what to believe anymore. I think you learned long ago to mask your emotions and that's how you always appear calm."

Surprisingly Evanderth stood and came to kneel before her. He slowly removed his leather gloves and held out his hands. "I am not sure you will be happy with the answers you find, but it is time you knew the truth about me."

His pale hands that were always hidden within the soft, black leather gloves shook slightly as she stared at them. "Why do you shake?"

"I am nervous," he admitted without hesitation.

Kahlahnni tucked her hands under her thighs. "You have nothing to fear from me."

"I know that, but I need you to know that you have nothing to fear from me. There have been too many half truths and misdirections and I want you to trust me, and I don't think you will until you know all my touch will give you."

"I trust you."

"No, you don't," persisted Evannderth.

Lahnni paused and considered his words. No, she didn't trust him. She wanted to, she felt that she could, but he was right—she just didn't. He had used her and left her to Darria to do with what she will. Lahnni would be hunted now for her powers, always looking over her shoulder now it was known what she was capable of. He had done that to her.

His beautiful eyes looked at her, entreating her to take his trembling hands and know his truth, whatever that was. "Please?"

That was it, the deciding moment. His emotions washed over her and she felt his need for her to know him. His need for her to understand him and why he had done what he did. She couldn't resist that and she reached and took his hands.

Rapid images filled her mind as a surge of mixed emotions came to the surface. She let go of his hands and took a breath. "You need to relax. Take off your boots and come and sit with me," she ordered as she tried to ignore the main emotions she had felt from him. Love and duty.

He nodded and stood. While he took off his shoes, she moved further onto the bed, closer to the wall, giving him space to sit opposite her. He settled onto the bed, mimicking her crossed-legged sitting position. Once he was comfortable, he again held out his hands, and she noted they were steadier now.

"You don't need to do this," she told him.

His gaze was piercing. "Yes, I do. I have never wanted anything more."

She looked down at his hands, not able to meet his eyes any longer. She saw something in them that made her heart race and her insides flutter.

"I was wrong," he went on. "I shouldn't have left you in such a vulnerable position. I underestimated Darria's ambition."

Lahnni's hand reached for his as she asked her first question. "Why did you leave me then?"

As she had done on numerous occasions, she focused on what the feelings behind the words she spoke were. Words could lie, emotions did not. A picture formed in her mind of a woman with floor-length blonde hair, held back by a rose gold crown. She stood tall, dressed in a courtly gown of rich blue and she held two boys fiercely to her side. It was the same woman that Lahnni had seen in the vision she had had when rapport had been forced on her by Lady Darria. But instead of feeling jealousy and spite, she felt admiration and duty. Understanding dawned and she raised her eyes to look into his aquamarine ones. "You serve Queen Anzhellika." It was not a question.

"Yes."

"You wanted me to meet Lady Darria to see if I could uncover what, if anything, she was planning to do to her sister's children."

"Yes."

"It also gave you an opportunity to prove your loyalty to Lady Darria by bringing her something valuable."

"Yes."

Kahlahnni felt nothing but truth and regret from Evannderth. "Everything went to plan until I didn't tell her what she wanted to hear," she guessed. His underlying emotional response was not as clear to that statement. "What happened?" she asked.

His hands slightly trembled in hers and she squeezed them reassuringly like she did any client she did a reading for. "I had to choose." His words were barely audible. Evannderth let go of one of her hands and slowly raised it to her face. He gently cupped her jaw. "I chose you."

The wave of love was unexpected and powerful. Lahnni had felt nothing like it and she struggled against it and the fear it brought. It was one thing to experience her love for this man, but to have it returned in kind was something she had not been prepared for. He dropped his hand and Lahnni wanted to reach out and place it back on her face. She wanted to trust it, to drown in it, to never come up from the safety of that feeling. With the avalanche of love came images. Kahlahnni sitting in the back row of the supplicant's meeting when they had first met. His attraction instant and palpable. Kahlahnni being branded and his concern that something wasn't right. His reaction to seeing her brand and recognizing it for what it was, even when the priest didn't. His triumph at finding her and his fear of losing her when he found her passed out in front of the cave. *All his emotions jumbled together, hidden from her by something like her own emotional shield*, she thought to herself. Which immediately begged the question. How? How did he do it?

Kahlahnni asked the question. "How did you hide all of this from me? How did you know not to touch me?" She held his hand loosely. If he chose, he could pull away and only answer verbally. She wanted to see what he did.

Evan looked down at her hand and held it tighter. "My branding was as difficult as yours, but for other reasons." He said the words slowly as if it still bothered him. She caught an image of a large courtyard filled with people, all staring at him, a sense of anticipation building, and then outrage filled the gathered people. "I am the firstborn son of a Duke, born to rule over a large estate and many holdings. But the Gods intervened and when my branding day came I was branded a warrior, forever marked to serve the Royal family. It wasn't until later that day, when all the fuss had died down, did the priest who had performed the rite came to see me in my rooms.

Lahnni found a picture of a short-statured man with onyx black skin, and bright blue eyes come to the forefront of Evan's thoughts. "He told me to lift my shirt, and there on my lower right hip was a second brand, the one of royalty. I hadn't even realized it had appeared there; I was so concerned with my warrior mark and not carrying after my father. 'Only those with the double marking get the rare chance to train with the Elite,' the priest had announced, though I had no clue what he was talking about. 'You must pack and leave with me tomorrow. There are too few of you to risk,' he had then explained"

Evan lifted her hand and turned it over, pressing his lips to her knuckles. "I never lied to you, but I never gave you the whole truth. When I told you that it is suspected that in the Settlement the Roamer's train assassins and spies, it wasn't a lie. It is rumored to happen."

Lahnni nodded her head. "Though it is no rumor, it is truth. The Elite they are named." She remembered her time amongst the handful of men and women who she had trained with for a time. She gasped as understanding dawned on her. "That is why you know so much about the old ways of the Pomaikka and why you would recognize the brand." She narrowed her eyes. "And how you were able to hide your true emotions from me for so long, and in such close proximity."

"It wasn't easy." He groaned as if in pain, and another wave of his emotions passed over her.

She laughed for the first time since she had been taken to Lady Darria's. He loved her. And it all made sense.

"Do you really forgive me?" He lifted his hand and trailed a finger along the side of her face before tucking a few strands of her hair behind her ear. "I love your hair."

Kahlahnni took her hand back. She felt conflicted. She knew he felt remorseful, that he understood how what he did had changed her life irrevocably, but that didn't mean she had to forgive him. "What would you do if I tried to leave here?" she asked.

"I would let you go, but I would go with you."

"What happens if I ordered you not to come with me?"

"Then I would follow behind you."

"Why? Is your life not here, playing spy for the Queen?"

"Because I can't be without you." He swallowed hard. "That is why I came back to the palace of Lady Darria in the first place. When she ordered me out on the pretext of getting tea I knew there was something amiss. I gambled that she wouldn't truly hurt you as you were too valuable to her alive, that is your bargaining chip. They all covet your gift and want you for their own."

"Including the King and Queen?"

"They have always known about your abilities; there are accords between the royal family and Pomaikka that must be honored. However, they did and will continue to allow you to roam freely, if you wish, as long as you continue doing what the Roamer has asked."

Kahlahnni sat there and blinked at him several times as complete understanding of how monumentally naive she had been. "I have been spying for the royal family that whole time, haven't I?" Anytime she felt, saw, or came across something that was of concern, she reported it to the master of her longboat, assuming that he would refer it onto the Roamer superiors if he thought it necessary. She never once thought he answered to someone else.

"In the interest of full disclosure, you have been spying more for Queen Anzhellika. She is the real power. King Tommofey is torn between his love for Lady Darria and his duty to remain married to the now queen and to see his sons raised and his country prepared for when war comes to our shores again. The revelation that Lady Darria is pregnant will throw the court into disarray."

"And make my predictions even more sought after from all sides." Kahlahnni felt a chill. "Evan..." She spoke his name softly. "I was never really free, was I?"

"No."

A tear slid down her face as a heaviness settled in her gut. "I think I would prefer to be shunned than caged. Can't I just belong somewhere?"

"Lahnni, you do belong somewhere. You belong next to me." He reached for her hands. "Did you not hear me before? I chose you." He smiled sweetly. "I chose you over duty, over loyalty, over honor, over my vows, over the very safety of my nation. I chose you," he repeated.

The feelings she got from the skin on skin contact said that what he spoke was the truth. Complete, utter truth. "But why?"

"Because I love you."

"Good," she said firmly and he looked surprised.

"Good?" he questioned.

"Yes, because I have loved you since the moment you caught me a fish for dinner. And it would have been awful to go through life bonded to someone who didn't love me."

"Bonded?"

"It seems the most practical solution if you plan on sticking to your word and being by my side for the rest of my life. I can't be a Roamer and have a warrior following me around without it causing suspicion. As my bonded you can be by my side and there will be no questions."

All she felt through their connection was affirmation of his love and an image of them going through the bonding ceremony.

"So you forgive me?" he asked again, and she felt how important it was for him to hear the words.

"Yes, Captain Evannderth, now that I understand everything I forgive you."

She felt his tension ease and his eyes soften. "I love you with all of my heart," he whispered. "And there is naught I want more than to kiss you, but we have both been either locked in a room or on the run for several days without food or bath and I fear my breath alone may kill you after all I have done to protect you."

Lahnni laughed heartily. Her body tingled to be so close to him and she longed to reach out and pull his lips to hers but he was right, she probably stank more than him and there was no way that would be his first memory of their first time together. She was not a teenager overrun with hormones, she had waited this long, a few more turnings would be bearable...just. "It pains me to say it, but I agree."

He reluctantly let go of her hand, uncurled his long legs, and moved to the edge of the bed. "I will go and order food to be brought here and the bath to be filled." He waved his hand in the general direction of the large shadowed shape next to the fireplace. "You are free to leave this room, you will not be locked in. I would advise against it though as no one knows you are here, except a select few and we don't need people seeing you and gossip spreading. You are safe for now."

I am not certain I will ever be safe again, she thought to herself. *But then again, was I ever truly safe? As my reputation grew, there would always be people who wanted me to tell them what they wanted to hear and people prepared to do anything to know the outcomes of their schemes.* She didn't voice any of this, instead she just smiled and nodded. "I long for food and a bath far more than to explore a palace I never had any intention of ever seeing the inside of, but now I think that was incredibly innocent of me."

He caressed her cheek and smiled. "I won't be long."

Chapter 15

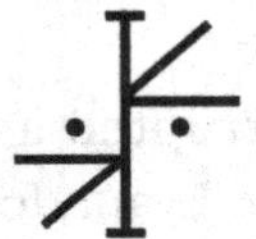

It had been several turnings since Evannderth had left her alone, and Kahlahnni had spent most of her time thinking. She had come to several conclusions about her situation and that she could either remain self-absorbed and continue to feel sorry for herself or she could become more like Evannderth and try to make the world better in her own way, not just profit from it, and occasionally pass on information if she stumbled across it. She could, with his help, actively look for what the Queen needed to know, but it all hinged on one thing...she needed to read the Queen and find out her intentions. Was Evannderth working for the greater good or did he just think he was?

There was a polite knock on her door and she answered. "Come in."

The same maid that brought her meal and supervised filling her tub now entered with a change of clothes and a mumbled apology for taking so long to find something suitable for a lady of her station.

Lahnni frowned but refrained from asking what station was that. "That is quite okay. It has been wonderful to sit in this robe and relax by the fire."

The maid went to the wardrobe and swiftly hung all the clothes she had brought with her. "Is there anything else you need, My Lady?"

Kahlahnni grew more confused. *My Lady? My station?* What was going on here?

A polite cough interrupted any further discussion. They both turned to see Evannderth enter. "That will be all, Peggy."

She curtsied deeply. "Yes, Lord Captain." She pulled the door firmly shut behind her.

"Lord Captain?" Kahlahnni raised an eyebrow at him.

"Peggy is my personal maid when I am in residence. She likes to call me Lord Captain, as it reminds all those in hearing distance that I am noble even though I bear the brand of a warrior. Queen Anzhellika thinks it is bemusing, so allows it. She says it is expedient as when I wear my uniform no one forgets I am noble born and when I wear court attire no one forgets I can kill them swiftly if they offer offense." He settled on the edge of the bed and winked at her. "I say it takes all the fun out of it if we warn people who I am."

Instead of laughing or making a light comment, Kahlahnni stood from her place at the small table, where she had been eating and idling looking out the window, waiting for the sun to rise and the day to begin. She was done with waiting, with him being polite. She untied the soft lemon coloured robe as she walked toward him, revealing the white satin shift underneath. It was though an invisible force pulled her along. All their problems and worries would be pushed aside, she needed him, needed him now. She craved to feel him on her, in her, surrounding her. It was as if the hands of destiny would wait no longer.

There must have been something in her eyes because he stood to meet her. His aquamarine eyes grew darker as his passion consumed him and she felt it pulsate from him as he let his shields drop and allowed her in. The emotions were intoxicating and she opened herself to them in a way she never had before. He took the final step toward her and their lips crashed together. Evan lifted her off the ground and Lahnni wound her legs around his waist. Her lips opened as his tongue searched for hers, and soon they were entwined in a delicate dance of sucking, licking, and twirling. Her groin tightened and her core burned at his touch. One hand cradled her arse while the other fisted her hair at the nape of her neck.

Slowly, he broke the kiss and made his way across to her ear where he nibbled her lobe and whispered words of love, making her spine tingle. Evan continued trailing kisses down her neck, his breath hot and his tongue rough. Without warning, a vision of Ambrosse licking blood from the cut on her neck made Lahnni cry out in fear. A vivid memory of Ambrosse's hot breath on her when she was nine, gloating and clutching her shorn hair, floated to the surface and she stilled like she had then, too scared to move. Evannderth instantly stopped kissing her and put her down gently.

Lahnni lifted her hand to the side of her neck, covering her scar. "I'm sorry," she whispered, almost choking around the lump that had formed in her throat.

"There is no reason to be sorry. Just tell me what is wrong."

"Ambrosse."

"Ambrosse?" he sounded puzzled. "I don't understand."

"Remember when I confessed to letting him die and I said that he had made my life miserable when we lived in the home?"

"Yes."

"We were in the kitchen, I was nine. We were eating breakfast and he told me to leave him half, as usual. I was defiant and deliberately ate all mine. I hated him telling me what to do and I figured I was safe surrounded by people. I was wrong." Her voice was flat, emotionless as she told her story. "Ambrosse was furious that I had again defied his wishes. While I sat there eating the last of my gruel, he came up behind me and told me that if I made a noise he would hurt me and then cut my hair off because he said he hated it, because I looked ugly and didn't fit in. As he cut it he cut my neck and as I bled he licked it." Kahlahnni closed her eyes for a moment, trying to push away the feeling of horror and revulsion that was coming from Evan. "No one did a thing. I sat there and let him cut the rest of my hair off, too scared at what else he might do." The feeling of horror turned to fury. Lahnni thought he might explode at the power of his anger.

"No wonder you let him die. I wish I could bring him back to let him die again." He lifted his hand and put it over the one she held to her neck. "I promise to stay away from that side of your neck until you say it is okay." He looked sad. "Is there anywhere else I should be aware of?"

"He broke my thumb on the day Cellecia took me away from the home." Lahnni held up her hand. "Thankfully, Lady Aisllyn had an excellent physician and she had no qualms about her staff getting good care, even the newly arrived orphan child."

He took the hand and she felt waves of understanding and love. He bent and kissed the palm of her hand, gently. "Do you want to stop?" He laid the palm of her hand against the soft pale skin of his cheek. "We have all the time in the world." His voice was patient, kind, all the things she loved him for.

"No. He didn't win then, he won't win now." Her stubborn side asserted itself, as it always did at these times. With deliberate movements, she withdrew her hand from his cheek and reached up to her shoulders and slipped the lemon robe off, allowing it to fall to the floor. She felt a surge of longing through their connection and grinned.

"What?" he asked.

"Kiss me..." She paused and stood on her tippy toes to reach his ear, and even then he had to bend down "Everywhere."

He took her hand back and took her thumb into his mouth, swirling his tongue around the tip before sucking on it. Fire shot through her and she let her head fall back, her mouth opening slightly. He released her hand and lowered his face to hers, resting his forehead against hers. "I love you, my beautiful bonded." And with those words he picked her up like he had so many times before and carried her to the bed, placing her softly in the center.

She wiggled up and put her head on the pillow. Kahlahnni watched Evan untie the top of his simple tunic before pulling it up over his head. She marveled at his hard, lean muscled chest, just as she had when he had stripped to go fishing, but this time she didn't hide the longing in her eyes. He kicked his boots off and they clattered along the wooden floor. Next came his trousers, which he let slide to the floor to join her robe. He left his breeches on, but it did nothing to hide his hard cock. Lahnni bit her bottom lip. "Take them off," she growled at him, surprised at herself for being so forward.

She had been with other men, but only the Elite Roamers, trained like herself and Evan to remain calm and centered, which maintained a shield around your emotions allowing you to focus. All of them had known her abilities and none had let down their shields to her and she had always kept hers as in place as possible while they had physical contact. The experiences had been pleasant enough, but when you always had to be on guard it took some of the passion away. Evan's willingness to let her in was intoxicating.

As he removed his breeches, as ordered, she sat up and tugged off her shift. As enormous and delightful his full erection was to witness, what drew her attention was the small mark on his hip. His royal brand. Her eyes remained on it as she crawled toward him. He went to move and she glared at him, playfully. "Stay."

Lahnni reached him and grasped his hips, slowly bringing her mouth toward his cock before she veered off and ended up planting a kiss on the brand. "My Lord," she whispered against his skin, breathing against his flesh, making him shudder. She sat back on her heels and reached for his left wrist, taking it and kissing his warrior brand. "My Protector." Kahlahnni pulled on his wrist and he sat down next to her on the edge of the bed. She climbed up on his lap and felt him hard against her. She wrapped her arms around his neck and kissed him deeply, feeling the blood rush to her core, begging for release. Lahnni broke the passionate kiss and pulled back slightly.

"My love," she declared. And with those words she sunk down onto him, making herself and him gasp as one.

Slowly she moved up and down, gently rocking her hips, finding their rhythm until she covered every inch of him and he moved against her in the most delicious way. He grabbed her arse hard but allowed her to keep her pace. It was incredible the sensation of him inside her body as well as her mind, and made her orgasm hard and fast. His pleasure at having her ride him was exquisite, but as she clenched around him, he maintained control of himself. Lahnni slumped against his chest, shaking as the aftereffect of her orgasm moved through her.

Without giving her further chance to pause, Evan wound his hand up in the back of her hair and gently pulled her head back. He kissed her with a complete sense of love, his soft lips drawing out her tongue. His other hand found her breast and caressed it before pinching her nipple, which hit directly at her core. She groaned in his mouth and ground her hips against his. He broke the kiss and trailed kisses down her chin, completely skipped her neck, and returned to kissing and licking at her collarbone before drawing his tongue over her breast and clamping his teeth around her nipple.

She found her own hand reaching up to twine itself in his blond, curly hair, adoring the way it felt. Lahnni moaned as he teased her nipple and pushed up into her. Evan unwound his fist from her hair and put it under her arse. Pulling his mouth away from her, he brought his other hand to her back. "Hold on." He grinned as suddenly he was lifting and flipping her onto her back. He managed to remain inside.

Lahnni brought her legs up to circle around his waist and pushed up, grinding against him. He bent down and kissed her on the nose before he reared up on his hands and knees. He pushed into her, hard, and she clenched against him, her stomach fluttered and her core craved more. With a wicked smile, he prised one of her legs off his waist and pulled it up over his shoulder, pushing into her harder and faster each time. Both of them groaned as their orgasms grew. He turned his head and kissed her calf as it rested on his shoulder before he grabbed the other leg and pulled it up to his other shoulder.

Evan sat up on his knees, no longer leaning over her, and pulled her up higher, tilting her hips and taking complete control. She surrendered to the moment. He ran one hand down her outer leg and across her stomach before coming to rest in between her legs. His fingers found her clit and began to move in a strong circular motion, causing her to widen her legs slightly. He did not let up his pace as he pounded into her, hard and strong as his fingers continued to help her build to climax. The sensations coursing through her body were pure bliss, and as she clenched the sheet beneath her she tumbled over the edge she had been holding onto and her body shuddered, exploding, with pleasure as Evan joined her. Together they spiraled, both yelling out each other's names with abandon, not caring who heard.

He let go of her legs, allowing them to fall on either side of his, and came down to rest on his elbows, kissing her deeply with all the love he felt.

"Now, that was worth waiting for," she murmured.

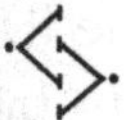

Turnings later they woke. Lahnni curled up tightly against his chest. Evan held her hand and stroked her thumb, the one that had been broken, and she found herself again reflecting, but this time it was on how different her life could have been without Cellecia in it. Over the four years since she had run away, she had had many lonely nights to go over her life and what may have been with different choices made.

"How stupid and self-centered I was back then." She turned to look at him. The sun was high and streamed through the window. "I was always feeling sorry for myself, always worrying about not fitting in. Forever fretting about not being accepted. I still do it now, it's like my default mode." Lahnni grimaced at him. Evan didn't say anything he just continued to stroke her hand and radiate acceptance. "They were trying to tell me something after the Branding Ceremony and I got so caught up in my anger at learning that they had hidden my identity from me that I wasn't willing to listen."

Lahnni remembered being trapped in the barn and telling Ambrosse that Cellecia and Captain Emmettin would believe her and she knew that to be true, then and now, but when Ambrosse had died and the barn had burned she had been hurt and confused by the revelation that it was true her brand had shown she didn't belong. "They kept me safe for all those years. Cellecia had always stepped in and helped. From rescuing me from Ambrosse in the Boarding House and finding me a safer place to work, to sending Emmettin to 'buy' me when Lady Aislynn had died. They let me live with them, be a part of their family, trusted me to take care of their children, and found me another safe place to work. Cellecia never attempted to hide or change my appearance, and it is only now that I fully understand how safe I was living with the Captain in the middle of town. Yes, I didn't fit in there and it had been incredibly lonely, but running away and not thanking them for all they had tried to do for me was wrong. They had risked their safety and the safety of their children for me and I never bothered to say thank you; instead I wallowed in my own self pity. And then I let them think I am dead. How cowardice I was." Her voice had grown small. She had never admitted that to anyone.

"They know you are alive, or at least they did. I do not know where they are now." He kept hold of her hand, but moved up into a sitting position, pulling her up to rest on his chest.

"What do you mean?"

"I lied because it seemed important to you to have no one know you lived, but when I went to town to announce you dead, your mother broke down."

For the first time, she did not correct him when he called Cellecia her mother because Lahnni finally could admit that that is what she had been.

"I made my report to the priest, put my sub-commander in charge, and then told them to keep moving to the next village as I wanted to stay behind and make certain funeral arrangements were made for Ambrosse as he was an orphan, and as his commanding officer I would make sure everything was in place."

She raised her eyebrows at him but said nothing.

"I went to your home to find your family distraught, blaming themselves for your death. I couldn't let them continue to believe you were dead. So, I swore your parents to secrecy, knowing both would never tell as they would continue to protect as they always had. Do you remember me telling you that the clothes I gave you were from a trunk of clothes the soldiers carried to give to the poor they encountered that needed new clothes?"

"Yes."

"I got the clothes from Cellecia. They had had them made as a gift for you as they knew your identity as a Roamer would be revealed and they wanted you to have something that was your heritage."

"Oh my God, I feel horrible." Kahlahnni felt ill. There were so many things she would have done differently.

"I didn't tell you to make you feel worse, I just wanted you to know the truth. I don't know why they kept your caste a secret and why they chose that town to raise you in, but it was obviously the perfect choice if they wanted to keep you away from anyone remotely connected to the Roamers and the outside world. Maybe they knew about your powers and were protecting you. Remember the first time you were near Pessac and you were completely overwhelmed with all the negative emotion? Maybe they chose such a tiny, insular town because not a lot happened and it stopped you from being swamped by all that emotion."

There were more questions than answers, but she had the one she needed the most. They had loved her and cared for her and Evannderth in his caring fashion had told them she lived. "You said you don't know where they are now."

"No, I returned to your town a little over a year ago, as I was in the area and thought I would check in on them. I knew I would see you again someday, and if the chance ever came up I wanted to tell you they were okay. They were gone, someone else was running the bakery, and no one could give me any details on where they had gone." He kissed the top of her head. "I'm sorry I couldn't be more helpful."

She sat up and gathered the sheet around her. She could feel his nervousness vibrate between them. It was odd feeling everything he felt, but helpful too. "You knew you would see me again?"

"Yes. Of course I did. I have kept tabs on you from the moment I left you. I still have a few connections in the Settlement and I wouldn't be much help to my Queen if my spy network couldn't keep up with the amazing Fortune Teller, Kahlahnni." He reached up and tucked a piece of her hair behind her ear. "And I was not going to go through life without seeing you again, even if it meant never talking to you. I had to see for myself that you had all you wanted."

She ran her finger down the side of his face. "I have all I ever wanted, now."

Chapter 16

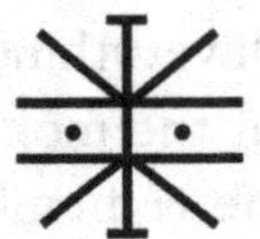

"Lahnni, what did you see when you touched Lady Darria?" he asked sleepily. She felt his curiosity with his arms wrapped around her. They had been hidden in her rooms for a sennight and it had been bliss. Exploring each other, sharing stories of their life, reminiscing about their time in the cave and forest together. It was a beautiful time that they knew would have to end, but they both clung to the fantasy that this could be their world forever.

"Lahnni, are you awake?"

"Yes, I was just pretending that we could be like this forever."

"Sorry, but I think we need to start thinking about what happens next."

"I know."

She closed her eyes and recalled the vision she had had at the hands of Lady Darria. Some parts of it were cloudy as they held less meaning now, while other parts she hadn't taken a lot of notice of seemed to appear strongly as she thought about it. A set of scales sitting on the dais between the two women and their children appeared in the image, something that she had not taken notice of before. When the specter of a person appeared standing behind and to the side of the queen and her sons, the scale had tipped that way, but when a different specter hovered near Lady Darria and her son, the scale tipped in the other direction. She explained all she had seen with this new thing added. "Everything is finely balanced and there is no clear way at the moment. There are players yet to be revealed." She remembered the changing of the light as the scales tipped. "I can be clearer with the knowledge that if Darria's son claims the throne there will be darkness and things will continue the way they are, and if the queen's son takes the throne there will be clarity. Things that have been hidden for too long will be revealed." She snuggled into his arms further but felt unsettled, there was something she was forgetting. A fleeting vision of a large stone arena filled her mind. "There is one more thing I saw, but I have no idea what it means."

She described what she had seen in that brief moment. "Do you know what that is?"

"What it is is hope." He kissed the back of her neck and a shiver went down her spine, her aversion to having her neck kissed had disappeared on the third day when she had discovered how pleasurable it could be when he had kissed the side she hadn't been cut on as an experiment. "I think you just described the Challenger's Arena, but we will need to speak to someone with more knowledge than me on the subject."

"Who would that be?" Kahlahnni was not truly paying attention as she felt Evannderth's growing desire both physically and emotionally.

"A Brother in the Order of the Seggar, he is an advisor on the Segarris council and trustworthy. I think it's time you met the queen too. We can't put it off any longer."

She pushed her hips back into his growing erection. "I trust you to make the right decision, but at the moment there are more pressing matters."

He nuzzled the back of her neck and slid a hand over her rib cage and onto her breast. "Thank you for trusting me," he whispered.

She reached behind her and took hold of his cock, slowly she squeezed and pumped him up and down. She felt the tip moisten with pre-cum and rubbed her thumb across the top and around the rim, he groaned softly in her ear. It was the sweetest sound and she loved to make him do it.

Evan fondled her nipple, pinching it hard and making her moan in response. His hand then slid down her tummy and over her mound until it came to rest in her slick folds. He swirled his fingers around for a moment before he slid them up her inner thigh and pulled her top leg up and over his leg. She was exposed to his fingers, but she kept a firm grip on his cock and continued to caress him. Evan moved his hand back down and pushed one finger inside her, she tightened around him and he slowly pressed in and out. He then added a second finger and Kahlahnni trembled as he pressed the heel of his hand against her clit, circling, while he continued to fuck her with his fingers.

Their breathing grew ragged and both were panting as they built each other to the peak of pleasure when Evan stopped his movement and Kahlahnni whimpered as he removed his fingers. He removed her hand from around him, and holding her top leg up he pushed into her from behind. Hard and fast, giving her no quarter as he slammed into her over and over. She clung to the sheets, holding her hips pushed back. Lahnni hooked her top leg around his and bit her bottom lip as she felt his hand slide down to find her clit and circled his thumb with ever-growing speed and pressure, making her moan as she built with him. She could sense his need, his urgency to fill her, and it turned her on like nothing else. The center of her being burned with desire and she burst into flames as her body stiffened against his pounding and hand. With one further thrust, he joined her as she clenched around him, both calling out the other's name.

As they laid there spent and happy, Lahnni felt something in the pit of her being, the very essence of her core. And for the first time in her life, she had a vision of herself. She was standing in a glowing doorway, the branding symbols blazing all around her, spinning in a circle of ever-increasing speed. Beside her stood Evan, his sword drawn and his face serious, blood seeped from a cut above his forehead. Kahlahnni stood with her black feathered cloak gathered around her, hiding her growing belly. She felt the urgency to protect it at all costs. She saw the baby's name emblazoned across the sky and knew it to be a girl.

With a tremulous smile to herself, Lahnni placed her hand on her stomach. She was pregnant.

T he tall woman sat on her throne, erect and cool. Her floor-length, blonde hair was braided and hung over the side of her high-backed, imposing chair. Her husband's seat was empty, as usual, and she held this audience session alone. Kahlahnni sat in the shadows of an alcove watching the proceedings. She was fascinated and sickened by what she witnessed. Sycophants and hangers-on simply sat around passing loud judgment on those who petitioned before the throne. These were most assuredly nobles and merchants who felt they were secure enough in their position that they could afford to offend anyone they wished. The Queen ignored their snide remarks as they were never directed to her, so she could do little about their behavior other than occasionally scowl at them. Kahlahnni on the other hand had grown tired of their comments, as she had once been on the receiving end of such horrid nastiness so she read each sycophant as best she could from her hidden seat and whispered to Evannderth, who sat next to her, exactly what each boorish man and woman were hiding. The information to be used at his discretion.

"You don't have to do this," he told her.

"I know. But I feel a need to pull these people up for their shallow bigotry and upper-class snobbery. I couldn't stop the people of Gennestenmont harassing me, but I can help the queen help her subjects better by removing these ingrates from her presence while she does her job." Kahlahnni was completely comfortable using her abilities in this capacity and on her terms.

They were interrupted from further discussion by a palace official banging his staff on the ground to gain everyone's attention. Lahnni couldn't remember what title Evan had given the man. Whoever he was announced in his clear baritone voice that Arch Deacon Zussya was here to see the queen on a most urgent matter. One of the sycophants sneered and leaned over to her friend and spoke loudly. "Probably here to beg for more food; look at the size of him. Most assuredly he has eaten all the rations they are supposed to give to those street urchins we donate to."

Before anyone could do more than gasp at the audacity of the uppity older woman in her bright orange dress with matching plumes in her hair, the Arch Deacon turned to her. "Hush now, Countess, your soul is in peril enough without adding my ire to it. You would do well to seek penance for your sharp tongue and dull wit." He continued along the wide aisle that led to the dual thrones and it took all of Lahnni's efforts to not laugh at the indignant face of the Countess and her pock-marked-faced friend.

Queen Anzhellika finished her business with the man standing before her, and then turned to the assembled nobles who all needed a life. "Gentlemen, Ladies, please forgive me as I must ask you to leave. I am certain that what news the Arch Deacon brings is not worthy of your time."

With little fanfare, the twenty or so nobles muttered to themselves, but all rose and shuffled out of the room through the main door. They were followed by the few citizens who had not been granted audience that day and would have to come back to try their luck tomorrow. Once the chamber had emptied, the queen moved to a side door that two of her personal guards stood in front of. "It will be more comfortable to speak in here," she announced.

The Arch Deacon walked through the door and only then did Evan move out of the alcove and escort Lahnni into the queen's private audience chamber. There were two guards already on the other side of the door and as Lahnni and Evan moved through, he ordered them to leave. Both saluted and left. Evan closed and locked the door behind him, earning him a raised eyebrow from the heavily bearded Brother of Seggar.

The room was filled with trinkets, piled on shelves behind the wide, light wooden rectangular desk. A large brocade-covered chair sat on the opposite side and Anzhellika stood beside it. There were several more of the same type of chair facing the desk, while a large three-seater lounge filled with cushions sat along one wall. The room was a riot of colors and not what Lahnni had been anticipating. Several large tapestries filled the walls, each a map of the three provinces that made up the mainland of Segarris, a fourth tapestry depicted a group of seven islands, in varying sizes, Lahnni assumed it was the Islands of Lobbregath.

Evan bowed deeply, first to Queen Anzhellika and then to the Arch Deacon, Kahlahnni quickly followed his lead. "May I introduce you both to my bonded, the Seer of the Pomaikka, Kahlahnni."

Both the Queen and Arch Bishop gasped, but she could tell that they were for different reasons. "It is an honor to meet you," she spoke to the woman that commanded Evannderth first.

"Seer Kahlahnni." Anzhellika inclined her head in a show of respect that Lahnni had not anticipated. "It is my pleasure to meet the woman who won the heart of my finest warrior." Evan had the grace to blush. "You may all sit." She turned to him. "Bonded?"

He cleared his throat and Lahnni felt his calmness ripple for a moment before settling firmly in place. "It was the right thing to do for many reasons. Logically, it gives me the excuse to be by her side and protect her. I can go more places dressed as a Roamer than I can a soldier or noble. People will underestimate me and that is never a bad thing. Lahnni is a powerful weapon that I have put in danger and I owe her my protection for that."

Evan paused and Arch Deacon Zussya interrupted. "All fine points, lad, but being Bonded is a lifetime commitment that only ends with death. The Pomaikka take their vows seriously."

"I love her," Evan declared to Lahnni's surprise. She had expected him to continue with his rational arguments. "I feel that the only way I can fairly serve my Queen and protect the woman I love and put in danger for the benefit of the queen is to declare to the world, and more importantly to Lahnni, that I will forever be by her side, loving her, and putting her first."

"It seems that your mind is made up, and I know better than to attempt to change it, so I will say congratulations and be thankful that you didn't try to quit your role to appease her for the harm you have caused. Though I want to resent you for choosing love over duty, it is nice to see someone in my council not crave power and want purer things." The queen smiled fondly at Evan and then turned her pale blue eyes to Lahnni. "I will say, though it pains me, that I will do whatever it takes to protect my children from my sister."

Kahlahnni inclined her head and thought of her child now growing inside her. "I would do the same, Your Majesty."

"I am still coming to terms with the fact that I now have proof that my husband betrayed his wedding vows and my sister carries his child. He has been gone half a year. Would you say she is further along than that?"

"Yes, but not by much."

"It seems she keeps secrets better than we both thought, Evannderth."

"She is very overweight, most people will probably think she is just getting bigger. This is honestly what I thought, and she sits down so often it is more diffi-cult to tell. They would have no reason to believe she is pregnant. Which works to your advantage," he observed. "Spread rumors that she has been dallying with one of her toadies; it will keep her occupied trying to figure out how to tell everyone it is the King's child until it is of an age where it won't be deniable as Lahnni says they all look very similar in some ways when they are older. She wanted me to fetch a priest so Lahnni could swear to what she had seen, but I got her out of there before it could happen. But it becomes another reason to keep my bonded safe."

"Very well, I will take your advice. Find me a suitable toady and have your people spread the word," Queen Anzhellika ordered.

"May I see your brand?" Arch Deacon Zussya asked, changing the subject and clearly wanting to move on to the topic that interested him, the fact that Kahlahnni was a fabled Seer of Pomaikka.

She had been expecting it and quickly rolled her sleeve up to expose the unique brand. Both the Arch Deacon and queen moved to inspect it but neither grabbed her arm and attempted to touch her in any way. To head off the questions Lahnni knew would come she spoke softly, already getting glimpses of things that were coming so strongly from the queen. "You fear for your sons, but also the sanity of your husband. You keep him busy chasing his tail and shadows on the Islands of Lobbregath." An image of the white bearded, brawny king falling off the side of a cliff into a churning sea below came to her. "You would do well to 'arrange' an accident. The cliffs of Lobbregath are slippery from what I see. Give him no chance to return and confirm her claim, this will keep her at bay for more years." The room stilled as Lahnni spoke words of treason, but she knew with unfailing confidence in her gift that she could speak the truth without repercussion here. "Arch Deacon, the second son will come to you confused. It will fall to you and him to find the truth in something that has been covered up too long. Only if the first son wins does the second son become free and understanding will come."

She stopped and looked at both of them. "I wish I could be clearer, but I have touched neither of you and this is what my gift wants me to know, but will reveal no more for now. Things must happen before the path becomes clearer sometimes."

"Which brings us to why you were summoned, Arch Deacon," Evan interjected. "Lahnni saw what I believe to be the Challenger's Arena in her time spent with Lady Darria. I was hoping you could tell us more about it and see if we can get a better understanding of her vision."

"The Challenger's Arena has not been used in generations. It is only required when there is a challenger to the throne. When the succession is murky." He studied Lahnni. "Tell me what you saw."

Quickly Lahnni outlined her vision of the women and their children on the throne, the hidden people on each side, and the royal robe and scales. Then she described the large stone circle building with its internal steps.

"I agree, Evannderth, it is highly likely to be the Challenger's Arena. I think that is what Darria is working toward. Those figures Kahlahnni sees on each side are probably the Challengers."

"The Challengers?" three voices asked at once.

"Yes. The contenders to the crown never enter the Arena, they have warriors stand in their stead."

"Makes sense," Evannderth said. "An heir would not be risked in such a way. How does it work?"

"It is simple. The named heir must find and name their Challenger once an official proclamation has been made from another that seeks to rule and has the credentials. The usurper must also find and name their Challenger. The Challenger's enter the arena and fight to the death, the surviving one's heir takes the throne and the vanquished heir is put to death and buried with their Challenger."

Lahnni had noticed that Queen Anzhellika had paled as Zussya explained what awaited her eldest son. "Kahlahnni, would you please do a reading for me, the same as my sister, and see what more we can find out? If anything new will turn the tide in our favor?"

"Of course, Your Majesty." Lahnni reached across the wide desk and offered her hands to the ruling monarch, who took them with greater care than her sister had.

Kahlahnni gasped as the image unfolded before her. Though she could feel a warmer personality than Darria, the queen was as ruthless and would do what she needed to secure her son on the throne just like her sister. The vision was the same. Everything so precisely balanced at the moment. Kahlahnni heard a cage door swing shut, it was her own fate tied into the vision. For the good of the people of Segarris, the firstborn must succeed, but for her own good, it did not matter. Both sisters would use Lahnni to their advantage and neither would let Lahnni be until their son sat on the throne.

Chapter 17

Her larger suite felt smaller than the room she had first woken in. The cage door she had heard as she read for the queen seemed to feel heavier every day. It had been a full month since that fateful day and Kahlahnni's greatest fears seemed to be coming true. She looked out the window and longed for the life she imagined she could have. Free from suspicion, free from people wanting something from her, free from people who wanted her to fit into their ideal of what the world should be like, and free from being a pawn in a game she didn't want to play. Lahnni was promised that she was free to go wherever she wanted, but when she left her rooms there were guards that followed her, for her well being she was told, but she wasn't so certain. And sadly, she soon realized she had nowhere to go. She imagined running away, but where would she go? The Roamers held allegiance to the Rulers of Segarris and that meant they would sooner or later be pressured into forcing her to use her abilities for the queen's personal goals.

Kahlahnni understood the want for the queen to keep her children safe, but she feared for her own child. Without realizing it, Lahnni placed her hand protectively over her womb, just like Lady Darria had.

Evan came and went as he continued his work for the queen and Lahnni had, for reasons she couldn't understand, not told him of his impending fatherhood. He continued to claim that he chose her over everything, but his actions weren't reflecting it, and even though it almost broke her to think about she would protect her child from being a pawn in a power struggle, no matter the cost, and that included the love of her life.

To take her mind off things that were out of her control for the moment, she had taken to sitting and writing all the details of the images she had seen regarding the sisters and their offspring. She also took notes of feelings she got, and ideas she had of how to best prepare for the future for the best outcome. She wasn't callous, or hard-hearted; she wanted the people of Segarris to get the ruler they deserved and her visions appeared to show the firstborn son in that light. Lahnni wanted to make sure he was as prepared for the role as he could be.

She tapped the paper as she reread what she had written the day before.

Train the firstborn in combat and strategy. Send him to the Roamers and see if they will help in his education. The second-born clearly needs to have a connection with Arch Deacon Zussya so have him study under the Brother's of Seggar as the King is not here to lead him in the ways of men, but also have him learn his skills with a blade. Don't allow either of them to be a sitting target. Send them away as they grow so Darria can't find them. Take them out of her reach until the Challenger for the first son is found.

Lahnni spent the remainder of the afternoon expanding on her notes and pretending her world wasn't crumbling around her.

As the sun set, she had the maid draw her a bath and leave a plate of bread, cold carved roast pork, honeyed dates, and nuts. A large kettle of water sat near the roaring fire so she could brew herself tea whenever she felt like it. She took the bath and washed her hair, knowing that it would take less time to dry if she sat by the fire and ate. After towel drying her hair, Kahlahnni took out a soft, red satin dress that she wore only around her suite; it was a Roamer shift dress and only worn in the company of your partner. It was slinky and cool against her skin and Evan always liked when she wore one. She loved the contrast of the bright red material against her burnished skin tones but was still a little cool, so draped her wonderful feather black cloak around her shoulders. She pulled her chair closer to the fire and brushed her long, soft curls until her hair was dry and it shone in the moonlight that now came through the window.

There was a polite tap at the door and Kahlahnni called, "Yes?" not bothering to stand up.

She looked over her shoulder as the door opened and a hooded figure stepped through, closing the door behind them. Kahlahnni felt an overwhelming wave of love and relief and knocked over her chair as she leaped to her feet to engulf the figure in a hug. "Heirrani, how are you here?" she asked the older man who had taken her aboard his longboat all those years ago.

He pulled his hood down and smiled his familiar grin at her, his two front teeth missing. "Your fella says he means to be bonded to you proper this time and I'm here to do the ceremony." He paused and his smile faded. "Unless ye be wanting to leave with me and return to Ohanaelle.

That can be arranged." He used the Pomaikka term for what the Segarrians called the Settlement.

Kahlahnni swallowed around the lump that had formed in her throat. She couldn't think of anything more wonderful than spending her life bonded to Evannderth, but if it meant putting their child in perpetual danger she wouldn't do it. A thought occurred to her for the first time and she pondered its significance. Had her parents been faced with a similar situation and that is why she was hidden away in a tiny town on the edges of nowhere so she wouldn't be found and used as she was being used now? Had her parents tried to avoid this very situation she was now in? Had they known what she would be and had tried to have her live a normal life? She turned to Heirrani and took his hands. "If I came back with you, could I stay until I gave birth and give the child to you to raise? But no one can ever know she is mine, or she will be used against me and I won't allow it."

Tears streamed down her face. It was a solution, not a happy one, but possibly the best one she could think of for her child. At least her child would feel wanted and know she belonged.

Before Heirrani could respond, the door opened and without turning Lahnni knew Evan had come in. She tried to wipe the tears away before he saw them, but he was too perceptive. He was at her side in an instant. "My bonded, why do you cry?"

"I'm pregnant," she whispered.

He held her tight and kissed the top of her head. Slowly he pulled his shield down and she felt his joy. "I know," he whispered back, as he resettled his calm demeanor.

"You know?" She pulled back from him.

"I may not be able to tell if Darria is pregnant, but I can certainly tell if my bonded is."

She laughed, for a moment her despair lifted, and she reveled in the love she felt from him. And in that split second she understood something clearly; she would not do this alone. Whatever happened, it happened to both of them and Evan would fight to protect their child as much as she would. She had been making herself miserable for no reason. All she need ever do was talk to him. She pulled his head down and kissed him until they were interrupted by a loud cough.

"Sorry. I got carried away." Lahnni winked at Heirrani.

"You always were a spirited young woman. I take it that ye plan is to bond with this man?"

"Yes."

"Good. And I am grateful to do this without the usual pomp. It should be between two people, not a spectacle, just because it is rare." Heirrani turned to Evan. "Did you bring what I asked for?"

Evan nodded and drew out a short, stout brown bottle from inside his cloak. He handed it to the elderly man who opened the bottle and took a long swig before wiping his mouth with his sleeve.

Lahnni frowned. "I don't remember that being part of the ceremony?"

"It ain't. It's payment for having to haul my old arse through the palace and all the lies I had to tell to get here with this." He drew out a black sash from his vest pocket and unfurled it. The sash had the branding symbol of the Roamers embroidered into it with silver thread. "Had to have this specially made for you," he explained and held it up. Each end of the black sash had her rare branding symbol embroidered in a turquoise thread that was the same color as Evannderth's eyes. "It took some time, which is why ye had to wait here for so long. Had to keep it all hush-hush and find the right person for the job."

"My love, I need to tell you something." Evan touched her cheek, and she could feel his trepidation which immediately put her on edge.

Lahnni had already been feeling something building, an ever increasing need to decide their future. "Tell me."

"Darria has finally decided to act after my betrayal. She has issued a substantial reward to anyone that can bring her my head."

Kahlahnni felt herself begin to shake. "We must leave." The feeling of foreboding increased.

"She has also sent out a contract to have you found, kidnapped, and brought back to her alive." Evan's eyes showed how distraught he was at that statement.

Her hand's covered her stomach. "That cannot happen."

"I will be dead before I allow it, and we both know how hard I am to kill." He placed his hand over hers and she felt a rush of love and regret from him. "I have someone working on finding us a safe place without us having to be locked away."

"We may have to hide with the Pomaikka until the babe is born and she can remain there safe while we separate and hide."

Evan's ocean blue eyes were fierce as he gripped her hand. "I am so—"

She put her hand up to his lips to stop him. "Shhhh...you were working for the Queen, doing what is right for your nation. You had no concept of what Darria would do once she knew about me. You are trying to fix everything and I love you for it. Let us be bonded and then we will face the next challenge together."

Heirrani took another swig before he put the stopper back on and tucked the bottle safely in his vest pocket. "Face each other and hold out ye left wrist," he said. They both did what they were told, and without further instructions they clasped each other's hand, making certain their wrists touched, which meant their brands rested upon each other. Heirrani wound the sash over their wrists again and again. "Repeat, together: Your life is mine."

Kahlahnni looked up into the face of the man she worshiped and repeated the words, hearing them spoken to her as she said them to him. "Your life is mine."

"My life is yours."

"My heart I give freely."

"My mind is open."

"I am yours to command."

"I will always think of you first."

As the words were spoken the sash grew tighter, binding them together in the ways of the ancient Pomaikka. Usually, there was cheering and chanting as the words were spoken and the bonding completed, but this time was different. The tightening sash somehow stripped away Kahlahnni's barriers, but did not leave her exposed to the world's emotions, just Evan's, as his shields too were stripped bare. Lahnni saw them standing in a store, but nothing like she had ever seen before. It was stacked with colorful books as far as she could see and a large ancient mirror sat silently in a corner, hidden from view by several more shelves. Occasionally people walked past the aisle, but they were wearing clothing she had never seen before. There was something extremely alien, yet somehow not frightening about the vision. She had a sense of home that she had never felt anywhere else. She looked up to find Evan blinking at her and she understood that he too was seeing what she saw."

Heirrani's voice intruded upon the vision and they were pulled back to the bonding. "We are one, now and always."

"We are one, now and always," they repeated. As their final words faded the sash unraveled, releasing its magical grip on their wrists.

A knock on the door stopped any discussion of what they had just experienced. Heirrani pulled his hood up and moved to the side of the room and stood in the shadows so he wouldn't be easily spotted. Evan walked to the door and opened it a crack before opening it wide and allowing another hooded man to enter.

"There is a lot of secrecy going on today," commented Lahnni as Arch Deacon Zussya pulled his hood back.

"That there is," agreed the Roamer. "Time for me to go." He embraced Kahlahnni and kissed her forehead. "I wish your journey were easier, but I get the feeling that will never be your path." He shook Evan's hand and disappeared out the door without fuss.

Lahnni bent to pick up the sash that had fallen to the floor and rolled it up and put it on the table. They were bonded and she wished nothing more than to kick Zussya out of her suite and spend the rest of her life making love to her man, but the stress, worry, and an overlay of excitement from the Arch Deacon gave her pause. He was here for a reason.

"What is it, Your Grace?" Lahnni asked, cutting through the small talk.

"I think I have found a solution to your problem." His words were rushed. "I think I can put you as far away as you can imagine from those who would harm you and the child."

Lahnni was shocked. "You know about our child?"

"Yes, Evan came to me desperate. He pointedly told me that we needed to find a safe haven for you and this child. He brought this upon you and wanted my help to fix it. Though I serve the queen faithfully, I will not see her become a monster and use you, even if she thinks it is for the greater good. I will save her soul, even if she doesn't know it."

"Very well. Where would we go?"

"Further than you thought possible."

"I can imagine fairly far."

"Another world far?"

No one spoke, but Lahnni looked to Evan and she knew he remembered the vision they had just had. Now she understood why it had felt so odd and different from anything she had experienced. They had been shown another world. Though she could feel his startlement at the thought of another world, just like her own, she could also feel an unusual acceptance, like this was the right path for them.

She waited for him to say something. He caught her hand and kissed her knuckles. "Anything for my bonded and our baby."

"Yes," Lahnni agreed.

"Good. It is under the palace, at the back of the cellar where the cheese wheels are kept and no one bothers to go except the turner, who never ventures further than the end of the wheels."

"How is this possible?" Evan asked.

"It seems there is a portal, a gate between our world and another, that has been used from time to time to hide someone or have someone hide here. There have always been rumors in the towers of records but no one ever talks. I asked one of the Sisters, who cares for the records, to see if she could find any further information. She is a font of knowledge and it seems she had a good idea of where to look as it took her shorter than I thought possible to find the information I sought."

"Can she be trusted?"

"Yes. She was once destined to be my wife. We were engaged, but the branding called us both in another direction." A painful look crossed his face for a moment. "The Gods had other plans for us, but it didn't mean we stopped caring for each other." He sighed. "I will return tomorrow and take you to the tunnels."

"No, we go tonight," Lahnni insisted as she sat on a chair to pull on her boots. They did not have time for her to change. "Grab the essentials and let us go."

All she could feel was as if the world held its breath.

Chapter 18

The underground passage beneath the palace was cold as they hurried down the cobweb filled narrow stone walls. "Not, much further," whispered Zussya. He continued to lead the way, his large shoulders hunched forward as he hurried. Kahlahnni was in the middle with Evan bringing up the rear. She felt dwarfed between the two men.

Several turns later and they reached a round room with an arch in the opposite wall but it was blocked by bricks. It was a dead end. Lifting his torch higher, Zussya lit several round, low bowls that were around the floor in a semi-circle. "This is it," he announced as he moved to the blocked archway. "Do you see?"

Kahlahnni and Evannderth came to stand next to him, both looked up at the imposing arch. Finally, it registered what the priest was talking about. Across the bricks were the faint etchings of the branding symbols. "The brands are all here. Including mine," she looked at it with wonder.

"Yes. Now we open it. With us being of higher castes and Kahlahnni being one of the gifted we should be able to open it without the other castes being represented or the use of the staff." He pointed to a long narrow rod of wood with a golden pronged head at the end. In the center of the prongs was a large gem. "There is an incantation and other things usually needed, but I think your gift overrides the need, as from my research, when it has been used in the past a person with the gifted brand is never present. You are too rare."

"What do we do?" asked Evan. He glanced behind him, checking to make sure no one was coming. Even though Lahnni would warn him, his training relied on his instincts first, and she admired him for it.

"Put your hand on your matching branding symbol." As Zussya spoke, he reached out and placed his left palm on the Religious symbol. His brand glowed white for a moment before the light traveled up his hand and the symbol began to shine under his hand. He did not release his palm.

Kahlahnni watched as Evan stepped forward, and without hesitation placed his left palm on the warrior symbol, his brand on his wrist immediately blazing with white light and traveling up his hand to settle under his hand. Incredibly, the light from under his palm reached out and found the royal caste symbol and a light pulsed brightly from that point too. Zussya stared at Evan. "I wasn't expecting that."

Evan shrugged but turned to Kahlahnni. "You ready?"

She nodded and stepped forward, her Gifted brand glowing before she had even touched the wall. Her eyes widened with surprise and then understanding as, from her brand, light spread to the Roamer, Commoner, and Servant symbols. In reality, at one point or another, she was thought of and had been treated like all of those castes and had lived as them for a time. The arch was recognizing that. That left one symbol dull and lifeless—the Monarch symbol.

Lahnni felt the symbol under her palm begin to pulsate and the room brightened. Taking on a life of their own, the symbols moved within the blink of an eye to form a small circle around the latent monarch, they began to spin, causing an almost blinding light. The circle began to widen, and as the brands spun they drew the monarch symbol with it. A void formed where the bricks had been and Lahnni could feel the pressure building. They all took a step back.

"Are you sure you want to do this?" Kahlahnni asked her bonded.

Evannderth looked down at her, his wonderous eyes serious. "Yes. I chose you and I will continue to choose you. I put your life in danger by revealing your secret to the wrong person." His voice was filled with anguish.

She reached up and stroked his face. "I forgave you for that. You did it with the best intentions for your country. What is one person compared to the well-being of a nation?"

"I took you away from the one place you had that was safe and thrust you into danger."

"It may have felt safe, but it was never home." She stood on her toes and kissed him. "I understand now why I never felt like I belonged. It's because I was looking for a place to belong when in reality it was you. You are my place, my people, and my home. I will go wherever you need to be."

"I need to have you safe. Our child is more important." Evannderth nodded to Arch Deacon Zussya. "Tell the Queen I am sorry for leaving her, but to heed the advice

Kahlahnni has given. You know as much as we do and will be able to help guide the children."

Evan took her hand and looked at the shimmering portal within the arch. "Let us find a place where we both belong and can be safe."

Lahnni had nothing more to add. She had voiced all she wanted to. It was time to go and start a new life where she would be safe and be like everyone else. She looked at the portal and knew with every bit of her power that what lay beyond was her place, where she would just be Kahlahnni. The thought was intoxicating.

She let go of her bonded's hand and hurried to Zussya. He embraced her and she allowed herself to feel his reluctance to let her go, but also his understanding. "Take care of her," he said quietly as he bent to kiss Lahnni's cheek.

"I will," Evannderth answered as he gripped his hand in parting.

"A last gift for you both." He held out a small cloth sack that Evannderth took.

"Thank you."

Lahnni felt a sense of urgency overcome her and she swallowed hard, suddenly frightened. "If we don't go now, we will not be able to go ever."

Evannderth studied her for a moment, and she hoped he could understand by her eyes how rapidly the feeling was growing. "Then let us leave." He picked up both his and her carry packs and hoisted them onto his shoulder before he held out his hand.

She took it and squeezed tight. "Together?" she asked.

"Together." He smiled and they both stepped through the portal.

Epilogue

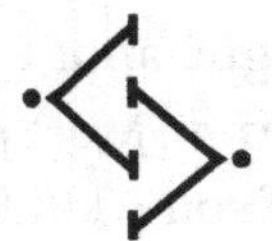

The beautiful, deadly blade thudded into its intended target.

"Well done, Fiaffia," Evannderth congratulated the young girl. It was his special nickname for her.

She looked up at him and smiled. Her pretty brown eyes were so much like her mother's. "Dad, do you think we can start learning the staff today?"

"I told you when you turn ten. Every year we add a weapon to your arsenal," he gently reminded.

"But I turn ten in three days. Surely a few days early won't matter."

"Cutting corners in training always matters."

She screwed her cute nose up at him and sighed heavily, full of drama, as only a ten-year-old can be, but she didn't argue. Instead, she walked across the dojo floor and retrieved the two blue metal blades from their target, and headed back to her mark. "Can we make the next few days more interesting then?" she asked, her voice full of sass.

He raised a blond eyebrow at her and hid his smirk. "How would you like to do that?"

"Can I practice throwing them blindfolded?"

Evannderth laughed. "When we get home. Not in the dojo."

Home was now a large expanse of land that sat nestled in the foothills of a mountain range on the outskirts of a city called Melbourne, in a country called Australia, on a world named Earth. It still made Evannderth's mind boggle when he thought about where they were and where they had come from. Most people assumed he was from Europe, Nordic of some kind, Kahlahnni was harder to place, but many assumed Egyptian, though her name didn't match that assumption.

It didn't matter though, all that did was that they were safe. Kahlahnni was safe and couldn't be forced to use her abilities to suit people's self-interests. He had caused her to have to flee her home and he would forever feel guilty for it. Their daughter was safe and couldn't be used to make either of them do anything they didn't want to. They were together and their daughter would grow up knowing she belonged, something Lahnni always longed for.

But each day Evannderth trained their daughter because even though Kahlahnni's visions no longer came, a sense of urgency continued to bother her, and she would wake every morning with the same words. Something was coming and their daughter must be ready.

She must be lethal.

This story continues in
Lethal
Book 2
Right to Rule Series

**He will fight to win her heart.
She must fight to win his throne.**

Prince Harlonngraith is on a quest to find his Champion, but could this soft spoken, aspiring author truly be it? His country stands on the brink of war and the wrong decision could mean the death of everything he loves. Was the Seer right? Is this mystery girl the one for him and his nation or has there been a terrible mistake?

Marra has lived a sheltered life; the only exciting things to ever happen to her are what she writes in her stories. But lately, her vivid dreams feel more real and her parents whispered private conversations are seeming more urgent. Something is coming. Now, she can only hope that when it happens, she will be lethal enough to survive her fate.

A portal fantasy romance, full of intrigue, secrets and steam.

Excerpt from Lethal

Harlonngraith's body responded, his cock growing hard as they kissed. It started off slowly and gently but soon turned to deeper kisses with their tongues joining and his body begging for him to take control and peel her clothes off so he could kiss every inch of her. He broke the kiss. "Marra," he said roughly, barely holding on to his senses. "Everyone can see us."

He watched with mild bemusement as she turned her head to the side to confirm it was still in fact the middle of the afternoon and they were clearly able to be seen through the large dojo windows by anyone who walked by. "I am most tempted to say screw it, I don't care," she confessed.

"I don't think Evan would be happy with either of us if we continued to canoodle on the mat for everyone to see."

"Canoodle?" She giggled. "Okay, no more canoodling. Let me up."

Harlonngraith moved to allow Marra to get up and deliberately groaned loudly.

"What's wrong?" she asked, her face filled with genuine concern.

"Would you believe that I was attacked by a jealous wench and my ribs hurt?" he asked innocently, hoping he had gauged her mood right.

"Unheard of. Absolutely not possible. You are so strong and tall, how could a mere woman ever hurt you?"

"I think you could easily kill me, if you chose to," he said casually. Marra laughed as she moved to gather her things. Harlonngraith stood in the center of the mat grappling with the implications of what he had said. She could kill him, easily if she chose. Yes, he had beaten her that first time they sparred, but there was something that made him feel like the truth had been revealed. There was a dawning that perhaps Marra was indeed his Champion. But instead of feeling triumphant, Harley felt nauseous. He hoped he had it wrong.

Warrior Brand

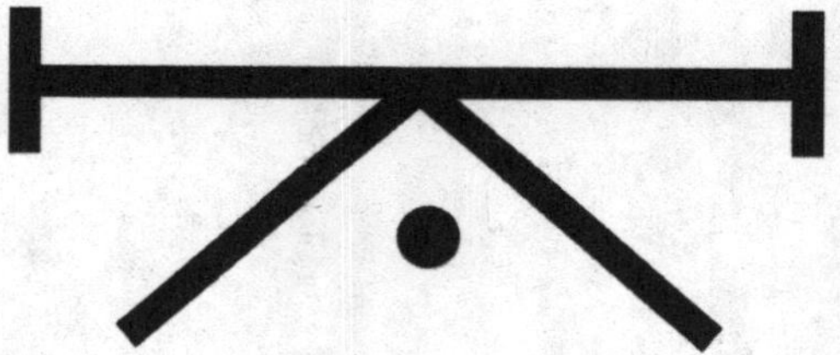

Religious Brand

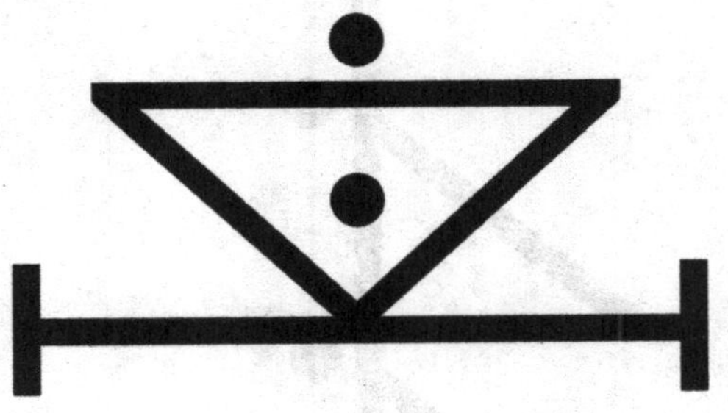

Commoner Brand

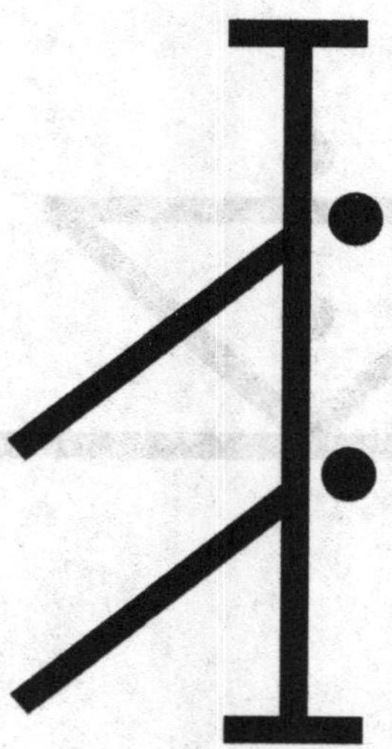

Servant Brand

Roamer Brand

Gifted Brand

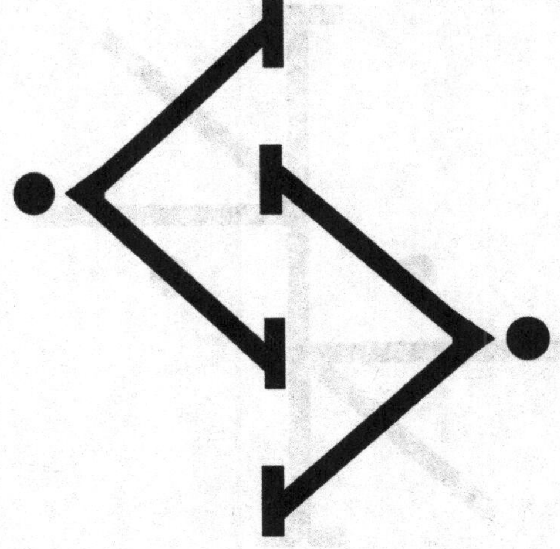

Noble Brand

Monarch Brand

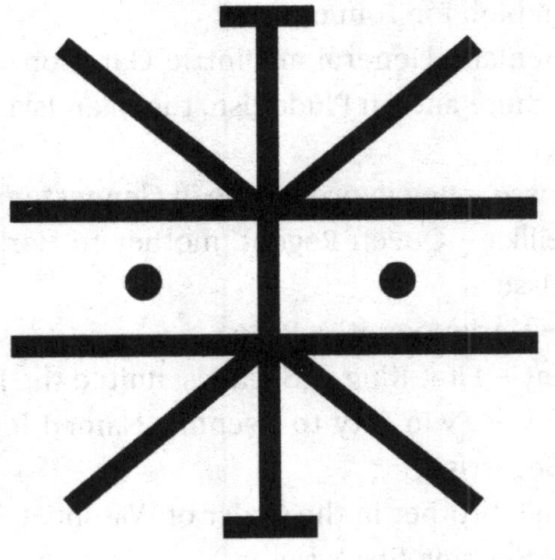

Glossary

Aislynn – Lady of Burrop.

Albertinne (Captain) - Leading the group finding the Champion for Tommofey.

Alloshenka - General at Binttle Garrison - runs the outpost there and on Pluddgish, the mian Island of Lobbregath.

Ambrosse – Boy in orphanage in Gennestenmont.

Anzhellika – Queen Regent, mother to Harlonngraith and Platisse.

Arris – Harlonngraith's Page.

Arsenny – First King of Segarris, united the Provinces.

Arsenny – Twin City to Csennia. Named for the first king of Segarris.

Arttem – Brother in the Order of Wasshu.

Aviva - Servant, Shai's sister.

Binttle - Town in the North East of Segarris in the Province of Jaggiron. Overlooks the Islands of Lobbregath.

Cellecia – Guardian of Kahlahnni. Wife of Emmettin. Mother of Margueritte, Mechelle, and Mattilde.

Channing – Lord of Burrop.

Correntin – Sergeant in Segarrin army.

Csennia – Twin city to Arsenny. Named for the first queen of Segarris.

Daiisi - General Alloshenka's horse.

Dancing Boar - name of an Inn.

Darria – Once Queen, now Lady. Mother to Tommofey.

Darvell - Stablemaster in the garrison of Binttle.

Ellei – Pomaikkan woman.

Eltta – Pomaikkan instructor.

Emmettin Finnley – Former Captain in Segarrin navy. Husband to Cellecia, father of Margueritte, Mechelle, and Mattilde. Guardian of Kahlahnni.

Evannderth Durrand – Sergeant, then Captain in the army of Segarris. Bonded to Kahlahnni, father of Samarra.

Fabriolla – Sister in the Order of Seggar.

Fabbron - Drill Sergeant in Brinttle.

Fennkston - Mayor of Binttle.

Gallya – Samarra's maid.

Griggory - Tommofey's Page.

Harlonngraith – First born son to King Tommofey and Queen Anzhellika.

Heiranni – Pomaikkan instructor for the Gifted. Father to Lopakka.

Innessa – Sister of the Order of Seggar.

Ittaie – General in Segarris army.

Jaronnderth Durrand (Duke) – Evannderth's father.

Jossiner – Laundry owner in Gennestenmont.

Kahlahnni – Seer of Segarris.

Kveller Durrand (Lord) – Evannderth's younger brother.

Larrs – Anzhellika's personal guard.

Laurynnse - Groomsman for Prince Tommofey.

Lavee – Brother in the Order of Seggar.

Lopakka – Pomaikkan instructor for the Gifted. Son of Heiranni.

Lyubbov - one of the Servants at Binttle. Roommate of Aviva.

Malekko – Pomaikkan instructor.

Marggot – Worked in laundry in Gennestenmont.

Margueritte – Eldest child of Cellecia and Emmettin. Sister of Mechelle and Mattilde.

Mattilde – Third born child of Cellecia and Emmettin. Sister of Margueritte and Mechelle.

Mechelle – Second child of Cellecia and Emmettin Sister of Margueritte and Mattilde.

Nikkitta - one of the Servants at Binttle. Roommate of Aviva.

Ottilie - Housekeeper in charge of Binttle garrison.

Pattraic – Harlonngraith's servant.

Peggy – Evannderth's maid in the palace.

Pepper - Aviva's horse.

Platisse – Second born son to King Tommofey and Queen Anzhellika. Brother of Harlonngraith and Tommofey.

Pynnan - Warrior escorting Prince Tommofey.

Ripperedst - Village in Wasshun Province.

Ruby – Kahlahnni's Horse.

Russlongraith – King of Seggaris. Changed the Branding Ceremony.

Samarra – Daughter of Kahlahnni and Evannderth. Soul Sleeper of Segarris. Champion to Prince Harlongraith.

Shacram - Disc like weapon attached to a chain. Common to the Islands of Lobbregath.

Shai - Tommofey's Champion. Aviva's brother.

Shullamith – Priest of the Order of Seggar.

Sittiq – Brother in the Order of Seggar.

Toby - Tommofey's horse.

Tommofey 2nd – Former King of Segarris.

Tommofey 3rd - Prince of Segarris. Mother - Lady Darris, father - King Tommofey, half brother to Harlonngraith and Platisse.

Tommofey – Third born son to King Tommofey, first born to Lady Darria. Half-brother to Harlonngraith and Platisse.

Traiss – Inn Keeper's daughter in Gennestenmont.

Yalenna – Anzhellika's Lady-in-waiting.

Yesskia Durrand (Lady) – Daughter of Kveller, niece to Evannderth. Cousin to Samarra.

Zussya – Arch Deacon of the Order of Seggar.

About Taya Rune

Taya Rune is a writer of romance, a sucker for happy end-ings, and has a knack for asking people uncomfortable questions.

She is a USA Today Bestselling Author and a finalist for Romantic Book of the Year for the Romance Writer's of Australia. Taya has had her work published in many anthologies and publications.

Romantic Women's Fiction

Reflections of Love Collection
Also releasing on Radish and available in Audio format

Hannah

Samantha

Olivia

Chloe

Lacy

Grace

Reflections of Love Novella Collection Volume 1

(Contains books 1 – 4)

For more information on all titles head to tayarune.com

Acknowledgments

I would like to take a few moments
to say thank you.

To my children, thank you for
teaching me to let go of the small stuff. I am proud of you.

To my family, thank you for the
love and support you have shown me throughout the
years.

To my friends, the ones that have
my back and are forever in my corner – I cherish you.

To my editor, Rochelle J. Simas – IDK art.
Thank you for the kind words that
always accompany the return of my fabulously edited
manuscripts.

To my ARC, Street, Beta, and Proofreader Teams.
You are appreciated.

Follow her on your favorite platform:

Website:
https://www.tayarune.com

Facebook:
https://www.facebook.com/taya.rune.75

Facebook Group:
https://www.facebook.com/groups/tayasromanticreal
m

Instagram:
https://www.instagram.com/tayarune/

Bookbub:
https://www.bookbub.com/authors/taya-rune

Goodreads:
https://www.goodreads.com/author/show/21156065.T
aya_Rune

Pinterest:
https://www.pinterest.com.au/TayaRune

Taya Rune